Protests and Riots

Other titles in the American History series

AMERICAN HISTORY

Protests and Riots

Michael V. Uschan

LUCENT BOOKS
A part of Gale, Cengage Learning

Detroit • New York • San Francisco • New Haven, Conn • Waterville, Maine • London

LIBRARY OF CONGRESS CATALOGING-IN-PUBLICATION DATA

Uschan, Michael V., 1948-
    Protests and riots / by Michael V. Uschan.
        p. cm. -- (American history)
    Includes bibliographical references and index.
    ISBN 978-1-4205-0278-7 (hardcover)
    1. United States--Social conditions--History. 2. Social problems--United States--History. 3. Demonstrations--United States--History. 4. Riots--United States--History. I. Title.
    HN57.U83 2010
    303.6'20973--dc22

                                                    2009048370

Lucent Books
27500 Drake Rd.
Farmington Hills, MI 48331

ISBN-13: 978-1-4205-0278-7
ISBN-10: 1-4205-0278-6

Printed in the United States of America
1 2 3 4 5 6 7 14 13 12 11 10

Printed by Bang Printing, Brainerd, MN, 1st Ptg., 06/2010

Contents

Foreword

The United States has existed as a nation for over 200 years. By comparison, Rome existed as a nation-state for more than 1000 years. Out of a few struggling British colonies, the United States developed relatively quickly into a world power whose policy decisions and culture have great influence on the world stage. What events and aspirations drove this young American nation to such great heights in such a short period of time? The answer lies in a close study of its varied and unique history. As James Baldwin once remarked, "American history is longer, larger, more various, more beautiful, and more terrible than anything anyone has ever said about it."

The basic facts of United States history—names, dates, places, battles, treaties, speeches, and acts of Congress—fill countless textbooks. These facts, though essential to a thorough understanding of world events, are rarely compelling for students. More compelling are the stories in history, the experience of history.

Titles in this series explore the history of the country and the experiences of Americans. What influences led the colonists to risk everything and break from Britain? Who was the driving force behind the Constitution? Which factors led thousands of people to leave their homelands and settle in the United States? Questions like these do not have simple answers; by discussing them, however, we can view the past as a more real, interesting, and accessible place.

Students will find excellent tools for research and investigation in every title. Lucent Books' American History series provides not only facts, but also the analysis and context necessary for insightful critical thinking about history and about current events. Fully cited quotations from historical figures, eyewitnesses, letters, speeches, and writings bring vibrancy and authority to the text. Annotated bibliographies allow students to evaluate and locate sources for further investigation. Sidebars highlight important and interesting figures, events, or related primary source excerpts. Time lines, maps, and full color images add another dimension of accessibility to the stories being told.

It has been said the past has a history of repeating itself, for good and ill. In these pages, students will learn a bit about both and, perhaps, better understand their own place in this world.

Important Dates in the

December 16, 1773
Colonists in Massachusetts protest British taxation in the Boston Tea Party.

January 10, 1917
Members of the National Woman's Party begin picketing the White House to protest for women's right to vote.

1914
World War I begins.

July 1848
More than three hundred people meet in Seneca Falls, New York, in the first national convention dedicated to helping women win equal rights with men.

193[...]
In May the Bonus Arm[...] goes to Washington D.C., to demand ear[...] payment of a bonus f[...] World War I veteran[...]

July 27, 1919
The worst of more than two dozen race riots during the summer of 1919 against African Americans begins in Chicago, Illinois.

| 1700 | 1800 | 1850 | 1900 | 1915 | 1930 |

1861–1865
The United States is embroiled in the Civil War.

1918
World War I ends.

December 29, 1890
The Seventh Cavalry kills nearly three hundred Lakota Sioux Indians in the Wounded Knee Massacre.

July 4, 1776
The British colonies in the New World declare independence from Britain and form the United States of America.

1908
Henry Ford unveils the Model T automobile.

1929
The Great Depression begins with a stock market crash on October 29.

History of Protests and Riots

1939
Germany invades Poland, launching World War II.

August 11, 1965
The Watts riot in Los Angeles, California, begins.

1967
The United Farm Workers led by César Chávez begins a five-year-long boycott of grapes to win better working conditions for farmworkers.

September 16, 2007
Protests by people who both oppose and support the Iraq War are held in Washington, D.C.

June 14, 2009
Los Angeles Lakers fans riot after their team wins the National Basketball Association championship.

August 28, 1963
In Washington, D.C., 250,000 demand civil rights for African Americans.

August 1968
Antiwar protesters and police clash in Chicago, Illinois, during the Democratic National Convention.

August 16, 2009
Supporters of gay marriage hold "kiss-ins" in several cities.

1945   1960   1975   1990   2005   2020

September 12, 2009
National tea party protests take place across the United States to oppose the government's spending on recession recovery.

1989
The Berlin wall is torn down.

1964
U.S. involvement in the Vietnam War begins.

1973
The United States pulls out of the Vietnam War.

1945
World War II ends and the Cold War begins.

June 27, 1969
Gay men and lesbians fight police harassment in the Stonewall riot in New York City.

The Importance of Riots and Protests

Frederick Douglass was born a slave in Maryland in 1818. Eighteen years later Douglass escaped to New York, where slavery was illegal, and in the next few decades he became one of the nineteenth century's most powerful opponents of slavery. Douglass persuaded many people through his writings and speeches that the United States should abolish slavery, a practice that allowed southern whites to treat him and other African Americans as possessions instead of human beings. On August 8, 1857, Douglass gave a speech in Canadaigua, New York, about why it was necessary to fight so hard to end slavery. He said:

If there is no struggle there is no progress. This struggle may be a moral one, or it may be a physical one, and it may be both moral and physical, but it must be a struggle. Power concedes nothing without a demand. It never did and it never will. [The struggle can be waged with] words or blows, or with both.[1]

The North's victory in the Civil War in 1865 ended slavery, and Douglass's efforts to protest slavery led indirectly to that historic development in U.S. history. By persuading many Americans that slavery was an evil that must end, Douglass helped make it possible for noted abolitionist Abraham Lincoln to be elected president in 1860. Believing that Lincoln would make slavery illegal, southern states seceded from the Union and on April 12, 1861, began the Civil War by attacking Fort Sumter in a vain attempt to preserve slavery.

Douglass's conviction that it was necessary to fight for a cause he believed in has been shared by millions of other men and women throughout U.S. history. Their beliefs have led them to engage in protests, both peaceful and violent, as well as riots that destroyed property and injured or killed people. Their actions shaped the history of the United States, and the way its citizens live today.

Dissent and Protest

Riots and protests are different ways in which people express their opinion on a subject, either negatively or positively. This dissent is most commonly displayed in protests by people angry about something that affects their lives, whether it is an action by a government, an organization, an individual, or society in general. Mass gatherings and marches in which people speak out about issues, such as racial inequality, an ongoing war, or gay rights, have occurred regularly in the nation's history. The nation's capital has been the setting for scores of historic protests, such as the April 25, 1993, March on Washington for Lesbian, Gay and Bi[sexual] Equal Rights and Liberation. The protest drew an estimated three hundred thousand people who demanded the same rights as heterosexuals. Other common forms of protest include signing petitions and running newspaper and television advertisements on controversial issues like abortion.

Protesters burned draft cards to show their belief that the United States was wrong for fighting in the Vietnam War.

Many protesters have expressed their opinions on issues in creative ways. In the 1960s, young men who believed the United States was wrong to be fighting in the Vietnam War burned their draft cards. The cards had been issued by the Selective Service System, the federal agency that could force them to serve in the nation's armed forces through the military draft. Destroying the cards was not only an act of protest against the war but also a crime because every draft-eligible male was supposed to have an identity card. In another form of protest, people who oppose abortion line up along streets for miles holding up signs and photos that explain their beliefs.

In *Dissent in America: The Voices That Shaped a Nation*, Temple University professor Ralph F. Young explains that Americans have been singularly willing to protest for causes they supported or opposed throughout the nation's history. Young also claims that protests like those against the Vietnam War have powerfully influenced the nation. He writes:

> However we define it, dissent has been the fuel for the engine of American progress. Dissent is central to American history. Not a decade has passed without voices being raised in protest against policies and decisions made by legislators, governors, and presidents. Even before the United State was established, there was dissent.[2]

The Vietnam War divided the nation more than almost any other war in U.S.

history. Draft-card burners and millions of other antiwar protesters in the 1960s and early 1970s made history by convincing the U.S. government to quit fighting. As a result, it became the first war the nation had ever failed to win. But perhaps the most famous and significant protest that ever occurred was on December 16, 1773, in Massachusetts Bay Colony. During the Boston Tea Party, about two hundred citizens boarded ships in Boston's harbor and dumped tea into the sea to protest the British taxes that colonists had to pay on tea.

The protest was one of the pivotal incidents that led to the American Revolution. However, an earlier riot incited by the same anger over taxes also was key in moving colonists toward revolution.

The Nation's Riotous Past

In 1765 the Stamp Act required colonists to pay a tax on printed material, like legal and business documents and even playing cards. Since the colonies did not have representation in the British Parliament, the colonists had no say in whether or how much they would be taxed. The colonists believed it was wrong for Great Britain to tax them without their consent. Citizens in several colonies were so angry that they went on violent rampages, destroying the offices and homes of tax officials and even injuring them. There were so many riots that the British government abolished the tax.

Hundreds of riots have occurred since then in U.S. history. Many of them were due to disagreements over politics, while others occurred over social issues, such

A man protesting the Stamp Act. The Stamp Act Riots marked the beginning of a series of events that led colonists to openly revolt against British rule and culminated in the American Revolution.

as racial divisions between whites and African Americans. From the end of the Civil War into the first half of the twentieth century, racist whites in northern and southern states rioted scores of times against African Americans. In the latter half of the twentieth century, blacks in many areas rioted against whites who opposed their fight for racial equality.

Riots in U.S. history have been condemned because they result in deaths and injuries as well as widespread property destruction. But in *Rioting in America*, University of Oklahoma history professor Paul A. Gilje explains that some of those episodes of violence have helped shape the United States in a positive manner. Gilje writes:

Rioting is part of the American past. All too often riots are seen as brief moments of spontaneous collective violence that erupt unto the scene, but only temporarily interrupt the constant and peaceful pulse of American politics and society. Riots have been important mechanisms for change. In the story of America, popular disorder has expressed social discontent, altered economic arrangement, affected politics, and toppled regimes. Without an understanding of the impact of rioting, we cannot fully comprehend the history of the American people.[3]

The Stamp Act riots marked the beginning of a series of events that led colonists to openly revolt against British rule and culminated in the American Revolution. Despite violence and lawless activities that are associated with riots, such as looting, many other riots also have played key roles in shaping the nation.

Protest Is the U.S. Way

Civil rights leader Martin Luther King Jr. once said, "Somewhere I read that the greatness of America is the right to protest for right."[4] Millions of American men and women throughout the nation's history have shared that belief by protesting and sometimes rioting for various causes. By doing so, they have changed the nation in which they lived.

Chapter One

Degrees of Dissent

During the summer of 2009, a series of dramatic protests against health-care reform plans proposed by President Barack Obama swept the nation. The protests peaked in August when U.S. representatives and senators held town hall meetings so citizens could comment on plans to reduce the cost of health care and extend it to millions of people who could not afford it. Opponents of the plan flocked to the meetings to vent their anger about changes that would occur in health care if the plan was approved by Congress. At many meetings, protesters shouted so loudly that speakers trying to explain the plan could not be heard. In Ybor City, Florida, Representative Kathy Castor was drowned out by protesters when she tried to speak. The meeting was further disrupted when people in the audience began pushing and shoving each other.

Emotions were so strong on the issue that some people opposing the plan threatened some members of Congress. Some North Carolina residents showed their opposition to the plan by making death threats against Representative Brad Miller of North Carolina because he had not scheduled a public forum so citizens could discuss the plan. Representative Brian Baird canceled a town hall meeting in Vancouver, Washington, after he received death threats because he supported the plan. Baird canceled the meeting because constituents who supported the plan told him they would not attend because they feared opponents would harm them.

Baird said the hostility of people against the plan was spoiling meetings designed to educate the public. For some opponents, "it's not about showing up and having a real dialogue or discussing point A or B about the health care proposal," Baird said. "It's shout them [presenters of the plan] down, disrupt them and then post your video of

Internet Protests

The Internet has changed life in many ways for people around the world. In their book *Cyberactivism: Online Activism in Theory and Practice* authors Martha McCaughey and Michael D. Ayers explain how the Internet also has become a tool for protesters as well as a battleground of ideas. They write:

> From its earliest days, the Internet has been about networking; not just networks of wires and hubs but networks of people. Protests, too, are always about networks, usually networks of people who have a common interest or concern and come together—whether in a physical place, such as in front of a government building, or via a petition or other campaign. No wonder, then, that the Internet has been a useful site for social activism of many forms. [Small] and large networks of wired activists have been creating online petitions, developing public awareness Web sites connected to traditional political organizations, building spoof sites that make political points, creating online sites that support and propel real-life (RL) protest, designing web sites to offer citizens information about toxic waste, and creating online organizations that have expanded to do traditional RL activities. Activists have not only incorporated the Internet into their repertoire but also, ... have changed substantially what counts as activism, what counts as community, collective identity, democratic space, and political strategy.

Martha McCaughey and Michael D. Ayers, *Cyberactivism: Online Activism in Theory and Practice*, New York: Routledge, 2003, pp. 1–2.

that disruption on YouTube."[5] To avoid a dangerous situation, Baird set up a conference call on health care so people could safely phone in their questions and comments.

Health-care protests also were conducted in the newest political battleground—cyberspace. People on both sides of the issue posted statements, videos, and comments on Internet sites to explain their point of view or to alert supporters to come to planned protests.

Aside from the new, high-tech methods employed by people on both sides of the controversial issue, the health-care protests were no different than those that had taken place throughout the nation's history. Like all the other protests, as well as the many riots that have marred U.S. history, people who engaged in them were motivated by the same desire—to make their point of view known on an issue they deeply cared about.

Dissent and Civil Disobedience

Health-care protesters in 2009 shared another common trait with everyone else who ever participated in a protest or riot—they were not afraid to risk offending someone by expressing their point of view or by doing it loudly, rudely, or in a way that involved breaking the law. In 1869 Susan B. Anthony helped found the National Woman Suffrage Association to help women win the right to vote. In 1872 when Anthony protested that injustice by voting in Rochester, New York, she was arrested, convicted of breaking voting laws, and fined $100. Anthony felt that she had to go to such lengths, even committing a crime, to bring attention to the issue. She explains:

> Cautious, careful people, always casting about to preserve their reputation and social standing, never can bring a reform. Those who are really in earnest must be willing to do anything or nothing in the world's estimation, and publicly and privately, in season and out, avow their sympathy with despised and persecuted ideas and their advocates, and bear the consequences.[6]

Other women who defied authority to gain the right to vote included women who picketed at the gates of the White House in 1917 and were arrested for allegedly endangering traffic safety with their low-key protest. The dramatic efforts of Anthony and other women helped force the United States to change the U.S. Constitution in 1920 so women could vote. Both Anthony and those White House protesters were willing to risk arrest in public

Susan B. Anthony felt so strongly that women should be allowed to vote that she broke the law by voting in Rochester, New York. She was arrested, convicted of breaking the law, and fined $100.

protests to accomplish goals they believed in. They were acting out the philosophy of civil disobedience, which involves breaking laws people believe are wrong or breaking laws to protest something they believe is wrong. This principle was perfected by philosopher Henry David Thoreau more than 150 years ago.

In 1846 Thoreau was jailed for failing to pay a local tax in Concord, Massachusetts. He refused to pay the tax to protest

Thoreau Goes to Jail

In July 1846, Henry David Thoreau went to jail rather than pay a local tax in Concord, Massachusetts. The famous author, poet, and philosopher was protesting slavery and U.S. participation in the U.S.-Mexican War. Thoreau was only in jail one night before an unidentified friend paid the tax for him, and he was released.

Thoreau believed that citizens should oppose government actions if they believe they are wrong, even if they have to break laws to do so. Thoreau's belief has influenced many protesters since then, including Martin Luther King Jr. Thoreau gave a speech about his act of civil disobedience on January 26, 1848, in Concord, and a year later his speech was published. It reads in part:

I have paid no poll-tax for six years. I was put into a jail once on this account, for one night. [I] saw that, if there was a wall of stone between me and my townsmen, there was a still more difficult one to climb or break through, before they could get to be as free as I was. I did not for a moment feel confined, and the walls seemed a great waste of stone and mortar. I felt as if I alone of all my townsmen had paid my tax.

In order to protest the U.S. policy of slavery and the country's involvement in the U.S.-Mexican War, Henry David Thoreau went to jail rather than pay a local tax in Cambridge, Massachusetts.

Henry David Thoreau, "Resistance to Civil Government," *Aesthetic Papers*, May 1849. Available at http://thoreau.eserver.org/civil.html.

slavery and the 1846 decision by the United States to go to war against Mexico. He only spent one night in jail because an unidentified friend paid Thoreau's tax bill for him. Two years later on January 26, 1848, Thoreau gave a speech in which he talked about the principle of civil disobedience that he had used to refuse to pay his tax. According to Thoreau, it was better for people to break unjust laws than to follow them because the laws might harm other people. He explains:

> Unjust laws exist; shall we be content to obey them, or shall we endeavor to amend them, and obey them until we have succeeded, or shall we transgress them at once? [If the evil of a law] is of such a nature that it requires you to be the agent of injustice to another, then, I say, break the law. [I] do not lend myself to the wrong which I condemn. Under a government which imprisons any unjustly, the true place for a just man is also a prison.[7]

Thoreau's entire speech was published in 1849 under the title "Resistance to Civil Government" and since then has motivated many other people who protested for various causes. One of them was Martin Luther King Jr., the most famous leader of civil right protests in the 1960s. In his autobiography, King explains that Thoreau's writing convinced him he was right to fight for equal rights for blacks even if it meant breaking racist laws, like those which forced them to live under segregation in southern states. King writes, "No other person has been more eloquent and passionate in getting this idea across than Henry David Thoreau. As a result of his writings and personal witness, we are the heirs of a legacy of creative protest."[8]

As King notes, protesters since Thoreau have used his philosophy to challenge things they disagree with or believe are unjust.

Marches and Other Mass Protests

There is an almost unlimited number of ways people can protest things they believe are wrong. One of the simplest and most effective is to gather a lot of people in one place to show how many people agree on an issue. This can be done at public events like town hall meetings, at protest marches, or in large gatherings in which the assembled crowd listens to speeches about the issue they are rallying around. Labor unions have regularly protested low wages or other contract disputes by picketing, which involves marching in front of their employer's business while carrying signs stating their grievances. People protesting other causes also have employed picketing. Anti-abortion supporters, for example, picket medical offices and clinics that perform abortions not only to protest abortion, but also to discourage women from entering the building.

Some of the largest and most historic protests have taken place in the nation's capital. One such protest was the March on Washington held on August 28, 1963, in which people rallied against racial discrimination. Martin Luther King Jr. gave a speech to the crowd of 250,000 people, explaining his dream of a nation in which blacks would no longer face discrimination because of their skin color. In simple but elegant words that made many white people realize how racism harmed blacks, King said, "I have a dream that my four children will one day live in a nation where they will not be judged by the color of their skin but by the content of their character."[9]

Mass public protests are effective because they attract a lot of attention and can show how strong support is for an issue. Protesters also can display their collective strength by having thousands and even millions of people sign petitions or write letters to public officials for their cause, whether it is ending a war, allowing gay people to marry, or lowering taxes. However, protests by individuals or small groups also can be effective.

The Ultimate Protest

On November 3, 2006, Malachi Ritscher set himself on fire near the Kennedy Expressway in Chicago, Illinois. Ritscher killed himself to protest the U.S. invasion of Iraq three years earlier. President George W. Bush and other officials claimed the war was necessary because Iraq had weapons of mass destruction that endangered other nations. When none was found, Ritscher and many other Americans were angry. Ritscher left behind a statement that was published by the news media not long after his death. It reads in part:

[Judge] me by my actions. Maybe some will be scared enough to wake from their walking dream state—am I therefore a martyr or terrorist? I would prefer to be thought of as a "spiritual warrior." Our so-called leaders are the real terrorists in the world today, responsible for more deaths than [al Qaeda leader] Osama bin Laden. [I] too love God and Country, and feel called upon to serve. I can only hope my sacrifice is worth more than those brave lives thrown away when we attacked an Arab nation under the deception of "Weapons of Mass Destruction." Our interference completely destroyed that country, and destabilized the entire region. Everyone who pays taxes has blood on their hands…. Without fear I go now to God—your future is what you will choose today.

Quoted in J., "Malachi Ritscher: A Martyr for Peace," Chicago IMC, November 7, 2006, http://chicago .indymedia.org/newswire/display/74806/index.php.

Creative and Extreme Protests

Environmental activists have sometimes acted alone to try to stop construction projects they believed endanger natural habitats of animals. They will chain themselves to trees, gates, or bulldozers. People who oppose the use of animal fur for clothing have tossed blood or paint on people wearing fur coats. On November 3, 2006, in an extreme case of personal protest, Malachi Ritscher set fire to himself and burned to death on the side of the Kennedy Expressway near downtown Chicago, Illinois, to protest U.S. involvement in the Iraq War.

Protesters have found many creative ways to make statements about their beliefs. In 1960 blacks in southern cities staged sit-ins at white restaurants that refused to serve them; they sat in seats for hours without being served, and many were arrested for trying to order something to eat. Protesters who opposed the Iraq War and other armed conflicts have staged die-ins in which they pretended to be dead, with some wearing bandages or simulated blood to make them look more like real war casualties.

Some protest methods seem bizarre but they are meant to shock and provoke people. In December 2007 Art Conrad of Bremerton, Washington, showed his anger at what he believed was the commercialization of Christmas by nailing a Santa Claus figure to a 15-foot (4.6m) crucifix in front of his house. Conrad

Antiwar demonstrators stage a die-in in Los Angeles, California, to mark the sixth anniversary of the Iraq War on March 22, 2009. Throughout the years protesters have found many creative ways to make statements about their beliefs.

claimed, "Santa has been perverted from who he started out to be. Now he's the person being used by corporations to get us to buy more stuff."[10] The method Conrad chose shocked and angered some people but it won media attention for his claim that too many people viewed Christmas as a commercial event instead of a religious holiday.

Temple University historian Ralph F. Young claims that in more than two centuries of protesting, "American dissenters have achieved different levels of success [by] hammering away at the powers-that-be until those powers began to listen, public opinion was swayed, laws were made."[11] Young says major victories achieved by protesters include unions being allowed to organize to better the lives of workers, African Americans having equal rights with whites, women having the right to vote, gays and lesbians having the right to marry, and the thirteen colonies being able to govern themselves. However, protests have often been marred by violence and sometimes have exploded into full-fledged riots.

When Protests Turn Violent

When the Democratic National Convention was held in Chicago, Illinois, in August 1968 to select the party's presidential candidate for the upcoming election, ten thousand people, most of them college and high school students, flocked to the convention in Chicago to protest the Vietnam War. The protests started out peacefully but developed into several days of full-scale rioting when police,

U.S. soldiers, and National Guardsmen wielding batons and shooting tear gas canisters used what many believed to be excessive force to control the protesters. In a similar manner, peaceful civil rights marches by blacks in the 1960s turned into riots when whites, including law enforcement officials who did want blacks to have equal rights, attacked protesters.

Such violence did not begin with the protests of the 1960s. Historian Richard C. Wade states, "Violence is no stranger to American cities. Almost from the very beginning, cities have been the scenes of sporadic violence, of rioting and disorders, and occasionally virtual rebellion against established authority."[12] Examples include the 1765 Stamp Act riots, the physical battles between labor unions and management in the nineteenth and twentieth centuries, and two centuries of racial conflicts between whites and blacks.

The first step to understanding the riots that affected U.S. history is to define the term, which is not easy because a riot involves more than an outbreak of violence. In *Rioting in America*, University of Oklahoma history professor Paul A. Gilje provides this definition: "[A] riot is any group of twelve or more people attempting to assert their will immediately through the use of force outside the normal bounds of law."[13] Even Gilje admits his definition is subject to interpretation because the level of force people use, whether it is shouting obscenities, beating or killing opponents, or damaging property, determines how much criminal conduct is involved.

Factors That Cause Violence and Riots

Riots, however, do not simply happen. Law professors David D. Haddock and Daniel D. Polsby claim that every riot springs from an event that creates strong emotions in people. In their article, "Understanding Riots," they write, "As word spreads of a conventional triggering event—whether it is shocking (like an assassination) or rhapsodic (a championship for a local sports team)—crowds form spontaneously in various places, without any one person having to recruit them."[14] An example of such an event occurred in New York City in 1969 when police raided the Stonewall bar, a popular gathering place for gay men, and began arresting people even though they were not breaking any laws. The arrests ignited lingering anger gays had about past mistreatment by police and made them fight back. This sparked the Stonewall riot, a landmark event in the history of the fight for gay rights.

Another factor that leads to riots are strong emotions that cause participants to perform acts they would never normally do, such as destroying property or beating or killing people. Such emotions can spring from anger over an incident like Martin Luther King Jr.'s assassination to

Demonstrators and police clash during a riot at the M.I.T. campus in Cambridge, Massachusetts in 1969. Rioters can become destructive and violent during such demonstrations.

the euphoria sports fans feel when their team wins a big game. When the Los Angeles Lakers won the National Basketball Association (NBA) championship on June 14, 2009, overly excited fans celebrated outside the Staples Center arena where the Lakers had played. Soon the fans' emotions were out of control and some were damaging police cars, throwing rocks and bottles at police officers, and starting bonfires. Gilje says that when crowds get pumped up by such strong feelings "the normal rules of society are put aside" and people are more prone to abnormal behavior. He explains that for people caught up in such a situation:

> rioting was not a daily routine. Each participant in a riot knew that he was involved in an exceptional episode of his life. Emotions and passions surfaced; people got carried away with what they were doing. Normally reserved individuals might find themselves cheering on the tarring and feathering [of another person], or, worse, firing away at the helpless victim themselves.[15]

Looting of stores during riots is an example of the kind of criminal action such strong emotions can lead people to perform. In the 1960s Vietnam War protests on college campuses often resulted in the destruction of school property. When many rallies ended, people leaving them were so angry over the war that their emotions led them to destructive acts like breaking windows,

smashing doors, and damaging other property. Many of the people who performed such acts would never have done anything like that on their own but became caught up in the frenzy of others and joined in the malicious destruction.

Another factor leading to violence or criminal activity during protests and riots is that some participants are people who are not directly involved in the cause that ignited the protest or riot. For example, a nationwide strike in July 1877 by railroad workers for higher pay and safer working conditions was marred by looting, property damage to railroad equipment and buildings, and violence. However, one historian claims that workers who went on strike were not responsible for most of the criminal activity. He says:

> The rioting had little or no connection with the strike, and few strikers were included in the mobs. Everywhere, but especially in Baltimore, Pittsburgh, and Chicago, the striking trainmen were promptly joined by throngs of excitement-seeking adolescents, by the idle, the unemployed, the merely curious and malicious.[16]

The addition of people who like to cause trouble makes it more likely that protests will erupt into riots. However, the anger people have about an issue is often enough to make ardent supporters of a cause act violently and do things they may later regret.

Time Turns Villains to Heroes

Like rioters, many people involved in protests have been condemned because the beliefs they expressed were unpopular with the majority of Americans. However, as time passed many of the beliefs protesters held became accepted by nearly everyone, such as the need to abolish slavery. And over time many protesters who were criticized or even reviled by national leaders and other citizens were transformed from villains to heroes. Martin Luther King Jr., who was bitterly hated by many white people while fighting for equality for blacks, is now honored with a national holiday on the third Monday of January every year. Susan B. Anthony, who fought for women's right to vote, also was honored with a U.S. commemorative stamp in 1936 and a dollar coin in 1979.

Chapter Two

Antigovernment Riots and Protests

Most of the protests and riots that have occurred in U.S. history have been directed against government. The nation itself evolved out of the dissent. Protests and riots during the colonial era, like the Boston Tea Party, led directly to the American Revolution. From this battle emerged the United States, a nation that was committed to allowing citizens a say in how they were governed. And not long after the nation was created, its citizens began using this power to oppose government actions with which they disagreed.

Shays's Rebellion

In 1786 Daniel Shays led more than twelve hundred farmers in an armed protest in central and western Massachusetts that became known as Shays's Rebellion. The rebellious farmers tried to seize control of local government to protest high taxes, a poor economy, and a financial system that had burdened farmers and

other people with huge debts they could not repay. A major aim of the protest was to stop courts from allowing lenders to take land from farmers or put them in debtor's prison if they could not pay their debts. The rebellion lasted from August 1786 to January 7, 1787, when a state militia arrested Shays and more than a thousand others.

Future U.S. president Thomas Jefferson was living in Paris in 1786 while serving as the nation's ambassador to France. Although many people were upset about the Shays's Rebellion because they thought it could lead to more civil disorder, Jefferson believed it was admirable that the farmers had taken up arms against a government they believed was treating them unfairly. In a letter Jefferson wrote on January 30, 1787, to James Madison, another future president, he explains, "I hold it that a little rebellion now and then is a good thing, and as necessary in the political world as storms

Daniel Shays leading a mob of protesters in an attempt to seize a Massachusetts court house during what has become known as Shays's Rebellion.

in the physical. God forbid that we should ever be twenty years without such a rebellion."[17]

Although two of the farmers were hanged, most of the protesters condemned to death had their sentences reduced, and in 1788 a general amnesty was declared for Shays and others who participated in the rebellion. Like many other protests and riots in U.S. history, Shays's Rebellion was beneficial because it resulted in changes that made the nation stronger and a better place to live.

New Rights for Americans

Shays's Rebellion was one of the factors that convinced members of the U.S. government that the nation needed a better set of rules for governing the nation than the Articles of Confederation, which the colonies had adopted during the American Revolution. The articles had failed to give enough power to the federal government to perform the tasks necessary to make the individual states a true nation, such as regulating commerce between states and having a unified court system. When the farmers revolted, the federal government had no power to intercede in state matters and Massachusetts had to raise an army to stop them. To correct that flaw, state representatives met in Philadelphia, Pennsylvania, in May 1787 to draft a new blueprint for a government that had the power to oversee the affairs of the new nation.

After months of vigorous debate, fifty-five delegates agreed on details of the U.S. Constitution on September 17,

1787. This historic document created the federal government as it exists today with an executive branch led by a president, a national judicial system headed by the U.S. Supreme Court, and a legislative branch consisting of U.S. senators and representatives from each state. The Constitution begins with a powerful statement claiming that any power the federal government has is derived from its citizens. It reads, "We the People of the United States, in Order to form a more perfect Union, ... do ordain and establish this Constitution for the United States of America."[18] It was a bold departure from how most people at that time viewed government. Most countries were ruled by kings or other members of royalty, whose power to govern was hereditary and not gained by winning the consent of the people they governed.

Despite the Constitution's claim that government gained its authority from its citizens, many people were worried that the Constitution gave too much power to the federal government over states and individuals. This issue resulted in a bitter fight over whether to ratify the document. To ease those fears, supports promised to include a bill of rights in the Constitution that guaranteed people basic freedoms that the new, stronger federal government could never deny them. Because of that promise, enough states voted to ratify the Constitution by June 21, 1788, and on December 15, 1791, the states approved the Bill of Rights in the form of ten amendments to the Constitution. The ten new rights gave Americans important freedoms that no other people in the world had at that time. The first amendment guarantees crucial freedoms. It reads, "Congress shall make no law respecting an establishment of religion, or prohibiting the free exercise thereof; or abridging the freedom of speech, or of the press; or the right of the people peaceably to assemble, and to petition the Government for a redress of grievances."[19]

The First Amendment to the Constitution ensures citizens that they have the right to disagree publicly with what the government does and demand changes they believe necessary, such as lowering taxes, ending a war, or giving women the right to vote. That right and the fact that any power the government has stems from the people and not from its elected officials have empowered U.S. citizens to freely, openly, and sometimes violently voice their displeasure with their government for more than two centuries.

Americans since then have never been shy about exercising their rights on nearly any issue imaginable. One of the favorite targets has always been taxes and how the government spends those tax dollars.

America's First Tax Protest: The Stamp Act Riots

The obsession Americans have with taxes and government spending actually predates the creation of the United States. In 1765 Great Britain created the Stamp Act, which required every sort of written material from legal documents to playing cards in the American colonies to have a tax stamp, or British seal, for which colonists had to pay to obtain. Colonists were furious they had not been consulted about the tax. In October 1765 delegates from nine colonies voted to challenge Great Britain's right to impose the tax. The colonies claimed the tax was "burthensome and grievous" and declared "it is unquestionably essential to the freedom of a people [that] no taxes be imposed on them but with their own consent."[20]

A group known as the Sons of Liberty employed violence to protest the tax. In Stamp Act riots in many cities the group damaged and looted the offices and homes of tax officials. Sometimes they tarred and feathered government officials, a process in which the victims were coated with tar and chicken feathers. This type of assault was painful and sometimes resulted in serious burns or even death for the victims. William Gordon witnessed the riots. He watched as hundreds of people ransacked the Boston home of Massachusetts lieutenant governor Thomas Hutchinson and damaged many other homes and buildings. Gordon recalls how the rioters "destroyed, carried away, or cast into the street everything that was in the house; demolished every part of it, except the walls…. [The] town was, the whole night, under awe of this mob; many of the magistrates with the field officers of the militia, standing by as spectators; and no body daring to oppose [them]."[21]

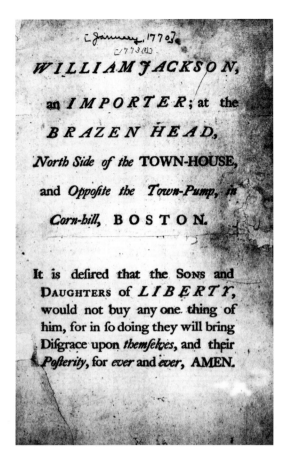

[January, 1770]
[1773(?)]

WILLIAM JACKSON,

an *IMPORTER*; at the

BRAZEN HEAD,

North Side of the TOWN-HOUSE,

and *Oppofite the Town-Pump, in*

Corn-hill, B O S T O N.

It is defired that the Sons and DAUGHTERS of *LIBERTY,* would not buy any one thing of him, for in fo doing they will bring Difgrace upon *themfelves,* and their *Pofterity,* for *ever* and *ever,* AMEN.

A document pleading with members of the Sons and Daughters of Liberty to not purchase anything from Boston tradesman William Jackson because he ignored the colonial boycott on British imports.

Women known as the Daughters of Liberty protested by boycotting British products like tea and promising never to marry a man who bought imported items. Historian Page Smith claims anger over the tax stamp was so widespread that it united colonists in a way in which they never had been before. He writes:

The evidence is in the rhetoric. In the space of a few weeks the colonists stopped talking of "our colony" or "our province" and began speaking of "our poor degraded country," and of thems-elves as "Americans." For the first time a current of sympathy and mutual affection flowed from colony to colony. Ideas and actions spawned in one province were quickly and enthusiastically adopted in another.[22]

Colonists were united so strongly that on November 1, 1765, the day the tax began, no items requiring tax stamps were sold. The boycott weakened Great Britain's economy so much that in March 1766 it repealed the tax, giving colonists a huge victory and showing them how powerful they could be when they acted together.

Taxes and Tea

Another historic tax protest was the Boston Tea Party on December 16, 1773. Angry that Britain had started taxing tea, a favorite drink of colonists, five thousand people gathered in Boston, Massachusetts, to show their displeasure. That night some two hundred Sons of Liberty disguised as Native Americans boarded three ships docked in the harbor and threw several tons of tea into the sea. The illegal act led to new laws to punish Massachusetts residents, including one that forced them to house British soldiers. Anger over taxes and the punitive laws spread throughout the colonies and began to convince more people it was time to end British rule of the colonies. Just two years later colonists began fighting for their freedom in the American Revolution.

The Boston Tea Party has been an enduring symbol of citizen outrage over taxation for more than two centuries. On July 23, 2009, the *Argus Leader* newspaper in Sioux Falls, South Dakota, published a letter from Douglas E. O'Neill in which he suggests that people should hang a tea bag from their car mirrors to protest high taxes. O'Neill writes, "I wish to start this symbolic movement on a national scale to tell others that I am protesting against the excessive taxes that Americans pay to the federal government."[23] O'Neill was a supporter of the Tea Party movement, a coalition of political groups that want the federal government to lower taxes.

A Shoemaker's Account

George Hewes was a shoemaker who participated in the Boston Tea Party in Boston, Massachusetts, on December 16, 1773. In the following excerpt, he describes how he and other men dressed as Native Americans and dumped tea from ships to protest a British tax on tea:

[I] dressed myself in the costume of an Indian [and] after having painted my face and hands with coal dust in the shop of a blacksmith, I repaired to Griffin's wharf, where the ships lay that contained the tea. When I first appeared in the street after being thus disguised, I fell in with many who were dressed, equipped and painted as I was, and [the men] marched in order to the place of our destination. [We] were ordered by our commander to open the hatches and take out all the chests of tea and throw them overboard, and we immediately proceeded to execute his orders, first cutting and splitting the chests with our tomahawks, so as thoroughly to expose them to the effects of the water. In about three hours from the time we went on board, we had thus broken and thrown overboard every tea chest to be found in the ship, while those in the other ships were disposing of the tea in the same way, at the same time. We were surrounded by British armed ships, but no attempt was made to resist us.

Howard Zinn and Anthony Arnove, *Voices of a People's History of the United States*, New York: Seven Stories, 2004, pp. 84–85.

Refusing to Pay Taxes

For more than two hundred years many people have refused to pay their taxes if they disagreed with government policies, such as allowing slavery to continue or fighting in a particular war. Julia Hill, an environmental activist, disagrees with the U.S. decision in 2003 to start the Iraq War. Instead of paying taxes, she donates the amount she owes in taxes to charitable causes like after-school and environmental-protection programs. Hill explains:

> I actually take the money that the [government] says goes to them and I give it to the places where our taxes should be going [instead of for a war]. And in my letter to the [government] I said: "I'm not refusing to pay my taxes. I'm actually paying them but I'm paying them where they belong because you refuse to do so."[24]

Refusing to pay taxes is an individual, nonviolent, form of protest as well as a crime, and Hill and other people who have protested this way have been charged with failing to pay taxes they owned. Penalties for this can include fines, forfeiture of property to pay back taxes, and even prison sentences. However, many protests against government policies have involved big crowds and violence.

Julia Hill says that instead of paying her taxes to the IRS, where they would be spent on war, she pays what she would pay to the government to other charitable causes. This is her form of nonviolent protest.

Protesting to Save a Tree

Julia "Butterfly" Hill is not afraid to stand up for what she believes in. During the Iraq War, Hill refused to pay federal taxes because she felt the United States should not have invaded Iraq. Hill, who acquired the nickname "Butterfly" as a child, also once lived in the canopy of a giant Redwood tree in California for 738 days to prevent loggers from cutting it down. She started the unusual environmental protest on December 10, 1997, because the Pacific Lumber Company planned to cut down the 180-foot (55m) tall tree which was more than six hundred years old. Hill remained in the tree she nicknamed "Luna" until December 18, 1999. She did not end her protest until the logging company agreed to preserve Luna and other trees within a 3-acre (1.2ha) area. During her protest, the environmental group Earth First! raised $50,000 in her name. The money was donated to further research on forestry. Hill, a cofounder of the environmental group Circle of Life, believes protesters can make a difference. She says, "By standing together in unity, solidarity and love we will heal the wounds in the earth and in each other. We can make a positive difference through our actions. Those things of real worth in life are worth going to any length in love and respect to safeguard."

Quoted in Circle of Life, "Inspiration: Julia Butterfly," Circle of Life, www.circleoflife.org/inspiration/julia.

The Bonus Army

The Great Depression which started in 1929 put tens of millions of people out of work and was the worst economic crisis in U.S. history. In 1932 veterans of World War I went to Washington, D.C., to demand payment of a bonus the federal government had promised them in 1924 for fighting in the war. The bonus was not due to them until 1945, but the men, many of them unemployed and destitute, claimed they needed the money right away to survive.

The first disgruntled veterans of the protest group that became known as the Bonus Army arrived on May 23, many carrying U.S. flags or signs demanding "Bonus or a Job." During the spring and summer, nearly twenty-five thousand veterans, including eleven hundred of their wives and children, came to the nation's capital to plead for the bonus. They camped at several sites near the Capitol and some of them occupied vacant buildings. The largest group of about fifteen thousand took up residence in an uninhabited swampy area known as the Anacostia Flats. They slept in shelters made from old lumber and boxes with roofs of scrap tin or straw scavenged from a nearby dump. Most veterans had little or no money and they survived on food donated by local charities. The group's leader, Walter W. Waters, a former army sergeant from Portland, Oregon, explains, "We're here for the duration and we're not going to starve. We're going to keep ourselves a simon-pure [thoroughly pure] veteran's organization. If the Bonus is paid it will relieve to a large extent the deplorable economic condition [of veterans]."[25]

The general public looked favorably on their plea for economic help, but some elected officials were not sympathetic. U.S. representative Wright Patman of Texas proposed a bill to pay the bonuses, which totaled $2.4 billion. On June 15 the House of Representatives passed it 211 to 176, but two days later the Senate rejected it 62 to 18. When members of the Bonus Army vowed to remain in Washington until the bonus

The U.S. Army Versus the Bonus Army

On July 28, 1932, President Herbert Hoover ordered the U.S. Army to force thousands of men, women, and children who were members of the Bonus Army to vacate the nation's capital. His decision resulted in the largest use of military force ever against U.S. citizens. An article in *Smithsonian* magazine describes how the soldiers forced the Bonus Army to leave. It reads:

[For] the first time in the nation's history tanks rolled through the streets of the capital. [At] 4:30 p.m., nearly 200 mounted cavalry; sabers drawn and pennants flying, [attacked] followed by five tanks and about 300 helmeted infantrymen, brandishing loaded rifles with fixed bayonets. The cavalry drove most pedestrians—curious onlookers, civil servants and members of the Bonus Army; many with wives and children—off the streets. Infantrymen wearing gas masks hurled hundreds of tear-gas grenades at the dispersing crowd. The detonated grenades set off dozens of fires: the flimsy shelters veterans had erected near the armory went up in flames. Black clouds mingled with tear gas. By 7:00 p.m., soldiers had evacuated the entire downtown encampment—perhaps as many as 2,000 men, women and children—along with countless bystanders. By 9:00, these troops were crossing the bridge to Anacostia. The troops swooped down on Camp Marks, driving off some 2,000 veterans with tear gas and setting fire to the camp, which quickly burned.

Paul Dickson and Thomas B. Allen, "Marching on History," *Smithsonian*, February 2003, p. 84.

Soldiers wearing gas masks advance on World War I Bonus Army marchers. The Bonus Army was protesting not receiving the benefits promised to them by the government after serving in the military

was due them in 1945, officials began to lose their patience. Finally on July 28, the federal government asked police to force the veterans to leave. When the veterans resisted, police shot and killed two of them but failed to force the rest of them out. President Herbert Hoover then ordered the army to remove the veterans in what became the most powerful use of military force ever against protesting U.S. citizens.

General Douglas MacArthur, chief of staff of the U.S. Army, gathered two hundred mounted cavalry soldiers, two hundred infantry soldiers, and five tanks to make the veterans leave. Major Dwight D. Eisenhower, who would later become the forty-third president of the United States, served as his liaison with Washington police and Major George Patton led the cavalry. That afternoon the cavalry, soldiers, and tanks charged into the areas where protesters were staying, clearing them out with brute force and the use of tear gas. Two babies died in the forced evacuation and nearby hospitals were overwhelmed with wounded, including women and children. When news footage of the forced removal was shown in movie theaters, people booed the army. The action was so unpopular with Americans that Franklin D. Roosevelt, the governor of New York who was considering a run for president, predicted: "This will elect me."[26] Thanks partly to anger over the callous treatment of veterans by the Republican President Hoover, on November 8 Roosevelt, a Democrat, won the first of his unprecedented four presidential elections. Although the Bonus Army was initially defeated, Congress authorized the bonuses two years later to give the veterans a delayed victory.

Americans have gathered in Washington, D.C. on countless occasions and for many different causes ever since. They gathered to protest racial segregation and discrimination, wars, and for women's rights. In 2009 angry protesters descended once again on the nation's capital to decry President Barack Obama's health-care proposal.

Dueling Health-Care Protests

On September 12, 2009, tens of thousands of people who opposed President Obama's proposal to revamp the nation's health-care system flooded the U.S. capital. They carried signs that said, "Obamacare makes me sick" and chanted slogans like "We the People." The protest was a culmination of heated protests at town hall meetings that U.S. senators and representatives held during the previous summer on the health-care plan, which sought to lower health-care costs and extend health insurance to people who did not have it. At the town hall meetings opponents of the president's plan often directed rude remarks at anyone who supported the plan, including elected officials.

On the same day, however, an estimated crowd of fifteen thousand cheered Obama when he discussed his proposal in Minneapolis, Minnesota. In his speech Obama asked, "Are you fired up?" and when the people in the audience shouted that they were, he responded by saying. "Yes we can!"[27] Obama had repeated those two phrases often during his 2008 presidential campaign to get people enthusiastic about voting for him. Obama used them again to excite the crowd at the rally in Minneapolis, the first of a series of campaign-style rallies he held around the nation to increase support for his health-care plan.

Most protests in Washington, D.C. have been conducted for liberal causes, like civil rights for African Americans. The health-care protest, however, was

Protesters stand next to a sign depicting President Barack Obama as Adolph Hitler during a demonstration before a town hall meeting on health care reform in Sommerville, Massachusetts, on September 2, 2009.

organized by several conservative political groups who claimed it was the largest conservative protest ever in Washington. In asking people to oppose Obama's plan, South Carolina Republican senator Jim DeMint proclaimed "Friends, this is a crucial battle for the heart and soul of America, for freedom itself."[28]

DeMint's claim goes to the heart of every antigovernment protest in U.S. history. Americans have valued the freedom to oppose government even before the United States became a nation.

John Adams, a leader of the colonists during the American Revolution and the second president of the United States, once said, "The revolution was effected before the war commenced. The revolution was in the minds and hearts of the people."[29] Adams meant that even before colonists began fighting Great Britain in 1775, they had started believing they had the right to protest government actions if they believed those actions were harming them. That belief has led Americans to continue to protest government actions for more than two centuries.

Chapter Three

The Fight for Workers' Rights

The annual Labor Day picnic in Cincinnati, Ohio, is one of the largest celebrations of Labor Day, the national holiday that honors workers. It is hosted by the American Federation of Labor and Congress of Industrial Organizations (AFL-CIO), which represents 11 million union workers in every conceivable job from miners to nurses and even professional athletes. In a speech at the picnic on September 7, 2009, President Barack Obama reminded a crowd of almost twenty thousand people of the many ways in which labor unions have helped make life better for all workers. Obama said:

We remember that the rights and benefits we enjoy today were not simply handed out to America's working men and women. They had to be won. They had to be fought for, by men and women of courage and conviction [who

demanded] an honest day's pay for an honest day's work. Many risked their lives. Some gave their lives. [So] let us never forget: much of what we take for granted—the 40-hour work week, the minimum wage, health insurance, paid leave, pensions [all] bear the union label [and] even if you're not a union member, every American owes something to America's labor movement.[30]

Even Labor Day itself was born from the long battle workers waged to gain better working conditions. The first Labor Day observance was in New York City on September 5, 1882. The Central Labor Union, which represented many unions, persuaded thirty thousand workers to take the day off and march to publicize their fight for better working conditions. Marchers held signs that said, "8 Hours for Work, 8 Hours for Sleep, 8 Hours for

A March of 100 Miles

When the twentieth century began, hundreds of thousands of children worked in mines, mills, and factories. Many of them labored sixty hours a week in unsafe, horrible working conditions. Mary Harris, an Irish immigrant nicknamed Mother Jones, was a legendary union leader who fought to establish labor laws to protect children. In the spring of 1903, Harris visited seventy-five thousand striking workers in Kensington, Pennsylvania. Ten thousand strikers were children, and many of them were missing fingers or hands from on-the-job accidents. Harris led some of the children on a march of 100 miles (161km) to see President Theodore Roosevelt to protest child labor. In the following excerpt from the book, *Dissent in America: The Voices That Shaped a Nation*, Harris describes the march:

> A few men and women went with me. The children carried knapsacks … in which was a knife and fork, a tin cup and plate. One little fellow had a drum and another had a fife. We carried banners that said "We want time to play." The children marched through New Jersey and New York and down to Oyster Bay, New York, to see [President Roosevelt], but he refused to see them. But our march had done its work. We had drawn the attention of the nation to the crime of child labor.

Mary "Mother Jones" Harris was a union leader who worked diligently to establish child labor laws in the United States. In 1903 she led a group of children on a 100-mile march to see President Theodore Roosevelt to protest child labor.

Ralph F. Young, *Dissent in America: The Voices That Shaped a Nation*, New York: Pearson Education, 2006. p. 374.

What We Will." They were protesting the twelve-hour workday that many companies required people to work. The New York event encouraged unions in other cities to hold similar celebrations and in 1887 Oregon, Colorado, New York, Massachusetts, and New Jersey made Labor Day a legal holiday to honor workers. On June 28, 1894, Congress passed an act establishing Labor Day as a national holiday. It is recognized every year on the first Monday of September.

In the more than one hundred years since Labor Day became a national holiday, unions have won many important victories for workers, including the standard eight-hour workday. Workers fought hard for better wages, job security, and better working conditions, sometimes in violent physical confrontations with police, soldiers, and thugs hired by the workers' companies. Those clashes resulted in deaths and injuries to workers and even members of their families. This long, bitter fight, which includes thousands of protests and hundreds of riots, has given workers a powerful position in society that early American laborers could not have imagined.

Exploiting Workers in the Industrial Era

In 1783 when the colonies defeated Great Britain in the American Revolution to win their freedom, three-fourths of the people residing in the areas that are now New England and the mid-Atlantic states lived and worked on family farms. By 1860 only 40 percent of the men and women in those states still lived and worked on farms, while nearly 1 million people labored in factories in cities. This huge population shift was caused by a growing scarcity of available farmland and the Industrial Revolution, the development of machinery and other new technologies that made it possible to mass-produce items like clothing, shoes, and wheels. Those two factors led people in rural areas and new immigrants to flock to big cities to find work in the new industries centered there.

So many people wanted jobs that employers could pay workers little, fire them for any reason, and make them work long hours under harsh, sometimes dangerous conditions. To gain leverage against their employers, workers banded together in unions so they could bargain with employers as a single unit. Unionizing gave workers the power to shut down operation of the companies by striking, which meant they refused to perform their jobs.

Some of the first workers to strike were women who made shoes and clothing. They were among the poorest paid workers because companies believed female workers were not worth as much as males. In 1825 the United Tailoresses of New York was the first women's union to strike for higher wages. Then in Lowell, Massachusetts, in 1834 the Lowell Female Reform Association, made up of women employed in factories weaving cloth, went on strike to protest a wage cut. "Union is power," the striking Lowell workers declared. "Our present object is to have

The Struggle Continues

Priscilla Murolo and A.B. Chitty are the coauthors of *From the Folks Who Brought You the Weekend: A Short, Illustrated History of Labor in the United States.* They claim that by fighting for their members, labor unions also have helped nonunion workers by setting standards for wages, hours, and better working conditions that all workers should enjoy. But Murolo and Chitty concede that unions have struggled at times to secure such benefits and are still fighting for them today. In their book they write:

> The history of American labor is one of constant struggle, against enslavement, impoverishment, and repression, for democratic rights, economic security, and dignity. The struggle has accomplished much. From the hours and conditions of labor to the regulation of occupational safety and health [rules] to social welfare like minimum living standards for old and young or equal opportunity [many] aspects of every-day life show the results of working people organized to advance their common interests. Despite these advances, the struggles never seem to end. [Labor's] cardinal role in this historic and democratic drama comes from the fact that labor is the engine of the [nation's economic] system. Labor really does create all wealth.

Priscilla Murolo and A.B. Chitty, *From the Folks Who Brought You the Weekend: A Short, Illustrated History of Labor in the United States*, New York: The New Press, 2001.

union and exertion, and we remain in possession of our own unquestionable rights."[31] The strike failed and the Lowell Female Reform Association had to strike several more times through the 1840s before finally winning concessions for better pay and a shorter working day of ten hours.

The Rise of Unions

By 1860 there was a union for nearly every type of job. However, their power was somewhat limited because they were localized in cities. But in July 1877, unions for railroad workers from many cities banded together into one large union and staged the most powerful strike up until that time in U.S. history. When Baltimore and Ohio Railroad workers walked off their jobs in West Virginia on July 14 to protest a 10-percent wage cut, railroad workers throughout several states joined them. Striking workers blocked trains from leaving railroad stations, shutting down rail transportation in a large part of the nation. The anger of the workers also led them to destroy railroad property and battle with police and military units sent to stop them. The August 11, 1877, issue of *Harper's Weekly* magazine describes the violence: "Scenes of riot and bloodshed accompanied [the strike] such as we have never before witnessed in the uprising of labor against capital. Commerce has been obstructed, industries have been paralyzed, hundreds of lives sacrificed, and millions of dollars' worth of property destroyed by lawless mobs."[32]

What became known as the Great Railroad Strike of 1877 ended in August after forty-five days when President Rutherford B. Hayes ordered federal troops into Pittsburgh, Pennsylvania, and other cities to quell the violence. It was the first time federal soldiers had been used in a labor dispute. It would not be the last as strife between workers and the companies that employed them continued.

The effectiveness of the railroad strike showed workers that a national union could give them more power because it could disrupt the economy on a wider scale. The Knights of Labor, one of the first important national labor unions, was created in 1869 but did not begin attracting large numbers of workers until after the railroad strike. The Knights represented both skilled workers, like carpenters, and unskilled workers, who toiled in factories. The union had some small successes, including a large railroad strike in 1885 but never became a major factor in national labor

Women weaving cloth in a Lowell, Massachusetts, textile mill. Because these women were among the poorest paid workers in the United States, they were some of the first workers to go on strike in the country.

relations. In the late nineteenth century, the Knights were eclipsed in popularity by the American Federation of Labor (AFL) and Congress of Industrial Organizations (CIO). The two groups merged in 1955 to form the American Federation of Labor and Congress of Industrial Organizations (AFL-CIO), the nation's largest combination of unions. These groups and the unions they represented waged a series of violent labor battles in the twentieth century to give workers more rights.

Historic Strikes

One of the most violent episodes in U.S. labor history occurred in Ludlow, Colorado, after eleven thousand coal miners went on strike in September 1913 because of dangerous working conditions and low pay. After being evicted from company-owned housing, miners and their families lived in a tent city in Ludlow for months while the strike continued. Mine owners convinced state officials to call out the Colorado National Guard because the striking miners were

A picture showing the aftermath of the Ludlow Massacre, in which the Colorado National Guard burned the tent city of strikers to the ground and murdered twenty-one people, including women and children.

beating replacement workers to keep them away from the mines. On April 20, 1914, there was a violent confrontation between miners and guardsmen. In what became known as the Ludlow Massacre, the guardsmen burned the tent city and fired machine guns into the tents. Twenty-one people were shot or burned to death, including women and children. When miners retaliated by destroying mine property, federal troops were called in to stop them.

Although the strike ended in October with no concessions from mine owners, the brutal slaying of women and children made national leaders sympathetic to the plight of workers. On October 14 Congress passed the Clayton Act, which legalized strikes, boycotts, and picketing by labor groups and President Woodrow Wilson— who had ordered federal troops to Ludlow—soon signed it into law. Legendary union leader Samuel Gompers hailed the act as "the industrial Magna Carta upon which the working people will rear the structure of industrial freedom."[33] Like the Magna Carta, an English document that gave citizens more individual freedom, the Clayton Act gave workers new rights in dealing with employers.

There was still a great deal of violence for two more decades involving workers. Many companies hired people to physically intimidate and even beat workers during labor disputes—they were called strikebreakers or scabs—and police and soldiers who sided with businessmen often used excessive force to break up strikes or labor rallies. University of Oklahoma history professor

Paul A. Gilje claims the violence was so bad that "to participants, America appeared on the brink of class warfare."[34]

An example of these conflicts occurred in 1937 during a sit-down strike at the General Motors (GM) plant in Flint, Michigan. The United Auto Workers (UAW) union, which had been started two years earlier, was trying to negotiate with the automaker for a new contract. GM, like many companies, refused to recognize the union. When that happened, workers went on strike but did not leave the plant. Instead, they occupied it, refusing to exit the doors. The action became one of history's most famous labor protests.

The Flint sit-down began December 30, 1936, and lasted until February 11, 1937. Family members of the striking workers and members of other unions surrounded the plant to show their support. At times as many as ten thousand people circled the plant. The supporters also gathered food and other supplies for striking workers. Police tried several times to clear workers from the plant, but strikers used powerful streams of water from fire hoses and threw auto parts to stop police from getting into the plant. The resulting loss of production hurt GM so much that it finally agreed to negotiate with the union.

The UAW victory helped gain wider acceptance for unions in general, which allowed workers in many different types of jobs to win the right to bargain as a unit for better wages and working conditions. Harley Shaiken, a University of California, Berkeley labor economist, claims the

UAW victory was historically important. He says, "[It] transformed GM, the UAW and much of the economy. That was a pivotal moment in labor history."[35] Shaiken believes the 1937 UAW victory encouraged millions of other workers to join unions which helped them win job security, higher pay, and other concessions that not only significantly improved their lives but also strengthened the national economy by giving them more money to spend on consumer products.

Violence in labor relations also began decreasing in the late 1930s because unions became more accepted by the business world and society in general. One reason is that during this period unions became a national political force as workers, spurred on by their unions, began voting as blocs for candidates who favored them. The Democratic Party supported unions more strongly than the Republican Party and was the chief beneficiary of those votes.

The Flint Sit-Down Strike

The sit-down strike at the General Motors (GM) plant in Flint, Michigan, helped the United Auto Workers (UAW) become a powerful union. Workers occupied the plant from December 30, 1936, to February 11, 1937, to force GM to allow them to become members of the union. In the following excerpt, historian M.B. Schnapper describes the historic sit-down tactic that workers used:

Throughout the 44-day strike, patrol, commissary, and sanitation committees maintained discipline. No smoking was allowed on production floors and liquor was prohibited. Supplies and food were provided by friends and relatives. When [General Motors] guards tried to enter some plants, they encountered a hail of soda bottles, coffee mugs, and iron bolts. Police who returned with tear gas were driven back by streams of water from fire hoses. The "Battle of the Running Bulls" [bulls is a derogatory name for policemen] was won without any violence. [The] success of the auto workers' sit-down techniques led to a wave of similar strikes in rubber factories, textile mills, and even department stores. Sit-downers in General Motors' factories made themselves at home despite the lack of normal conveniences. Car seats provided sleeping as well as lounge facilities. [Author] Upton Sinclair told a reporter "big business has been sitting down on the American people...I am delighted to see the process finally being reversed."

M.B. Schnapper, *American Labor: A Bicentennial History*, Washington, DC: Public Affairs Press, 1975, p. 520.

Unions are most often associated with urban areas because that is where most union members live, from factory workers to blue-collar office workers. But people who work on farms also have banded together to fight for social and economic changes that benefit them.

United Farm Workers

For many decades farm workers were the largest group of workers unable to start unions to help them bargain with owners of farms on which they worked. Most of these agricultural workers were migrant laborers who traveled from farm to farm to harvest crops like grapes and lettuce. These workers, many of the Mexican immigrants, had to accept whatever wages and working conditions growers offered them. Owners ignored labor laws that applied to other workers, such as limiting the number of hours they had to work each day.

This began to change in 1962 when César Chávez and Dolores Huerta began the National Farm Workers Association, which later became known as the United Farm Workers (UFW) union. Chávez, a Mexican American, simply wanted to improve life for farmworkers. Chávez explains:

I had a dream that the only reason the employers were

so powerful was not because they in fact had that much power, in terms of dealing with the lives of their workers at will, but what made them truly powerful was that we were weak. And if we could somehow begin to develop some strength among ourselves, I felt that we could begin to equal that, balancing their power in agriculture.[36]

Working conditions and wages finally improved for farm workers when Dolores Huerta and César Chávez formed the United Farm Workers Union in the 1960s.

Chávez is most famous for using a grape boycott to force California grape growers to bargain with his union so workers would have better working conditions. In 1967 when grape growers would not recognize the union, workers went on strike. To pressure the growers into accepting the union, Chávez began a nationwide campaign to get people to support his union and the boycott by not buying California grapes or products made from California grapes, such as wine. The grape boycott was one of the most-famous and longest product boycotts in U.S. history, and it was supported by millions of Americans who sympathized with the plight of farm workers. The boycott lasted five years and forced growers to bargain with the union, which allowed workers to obtain higher pay and more benefits.

Workers Changed History

Chávez used peaceful tactics in his campaign against grape growers, including several hunger strikes, to gain national attention. Riots and other violence, however, have often marred labor disputes in U.S. history. Historian Ralph W. Conant defends the disturbances because he believes they were a necessary part of the process of change the nation went through in labor relations. Conant writes, "The labor strikes that tore at the fabric of an emerging industrial economy for over half a century are in retrospect interpreted as constructive conflict which was directly responsible for the establishment of the bargaining rights of labor."[37] The right of workers to bargain with employers has helped both them and the nation become economically stronger.

Chapter Four

The Fight for Racial Equality

Racial strife has been one of the greatest causes of protests and riots throughout U.S. history. From the time the first English colonists arrived in the New World in 1607, white Europeans, African Americans, Native Americans, and Asians, have had trouble getting along. They also have competed with each other for control of the nation's land and natural resources, for jobs and other economic opportunities, and for political power. The nation's white majority has often used its political and economic power to discriminate against and dominate racial minorities. The tensions that have existed for centuries between various groups of Americans have often boiled over into violent protests, riots, and even full-scale wars. In fact historians David Boesel and Peter H. Rossi flatly state, "Of all the sources of civil disorder...none has been more persistent than race. Whether in the North or South, whether before or after the Civil War, whether nineteenth or twentieth century, this question has been at the root of more physical violence than any other."[38]

The group of Americans that has been subjected to racial violence and injustice the longest also was the first to inhabit the land that became the United States—Native Americans. From the time the first colonists arrived in 1607, they waged war against Indians to take away the future nation from its original inhabitants.

A Massacre and an Occupation

Wounded Knee is a tiny community of about 350 people in Shannon County, South Dakota. It is the location where two of the most historic events in Native American history took place—the Wounded Knee Massacre in 1890 and the Wounded Knee Occupation nearly a century later in 1973.

Two armed Native Americans stand guard during the Wounded Knee Occupation in 1973. Native American leader Russell Means said that the Wounded Knee protest was important in order to restore the group's dignity and self-pride.

On December 23, 1890, three-hundred-fifty men, women, and children of the Lakota band of Sioux began a 150-mile (241km) trek from their village on the Cheyenne River to the Pine Ridge Indian Agency so they could be with other Sioux living there. When they arrived on December 28, five hundred soldiers of the Seventh Cavalry forced them to camp at nearby Wounded Knee Creek. Government officials had given the order, fearing the Lakota would join Pine Ridge Sioux in an armed revolt against whites. The next day soldiers disarmed the Lakota and began searching their tents for any remaining weapons. When a shot was heard—no one

knows if an Indian or soldier fired it—the cavalrymen opened fire on the unarmed Sioux with rifles, pistols, and cannons, killing nearly three hundred people. American Horse, a survivor, describes how soldiers murdered women and children:

> The women as they were fleeing with their babes were killed together, shot right through. [After] most all of them had been killed a cry was made that all those who were not killed [or] wounded should come forth and they would be safe. Little boys who were not wounded came out of their places

of refuge, and as soon as they came in sight a number of soldiers surrounded them and butchered them.[39]

Nearly a century after the Wounded Knee Massacre, on the night of February 27, 1973, fifty-four cars drove into Wounded Knee, now a town on the Pine Ridge Indian Reservation, to begin one of the most famous protests in U.S. history. Commanded by American Indian Movement (AIM) leaders like Russell Means, about two hundred Native Americans occupied the small town for seventy-one days in an armed standoff with police, Federal Bureau of Investigation (FBI) agents, and members of the U. S. military. The occupation was staged to make Americans aware of the mistreatment of Native Americans by whites throughout the nation's history and to demand help for these people who were still struggling economically and in other ways. According to Means, the protest was important to Native Americans. He said, "We were about to be obliterated culturally. Our spiritual way of life—our entire way of life was about to be stamped out and this was a rebirth of our dignity and self-pride."[40] The protest ended May 5 when the Native Americans agreed to peacefully end the occupation.

The massacre and the occupation at Wounded Knee are symbolic of the racist violence white Americans have sometimes directed against Native Americans, African Americans, Asians, and other ethnic groups and the attempts by those minority groups to fight for the right to be treated as equals. No group has had a longer history of being subjected to racism by whites and fighting it than Native Americans.

Native Americans Demand Their Rights

For decades the action that took place on December 23, 1890, at Wounded Knee Creek was referred to as the battle of Wounded Knee. Historians now call it the Wounded Knee Massacre because the Lakota had no chance to fight the soldiers who had surrounded them. By either name, the tragic event was a turning point in history because it ended a three-centuries-long war between whites and Native Americans for control of the United States. From the time the first colonists arrived in 1607, they began taking land from Native Americans. Whites were able to do this because they had superior arms—rifles, guns, and cannons instead of bows and arrows and spears—and because the many tribes scattered across the continent were never able to mount a united front against the newcomers advancing westward from the Atlantic Ocean.

The defeated Native Americans were forced to live on federal reservations where they had little say over how white officials governed their lives. They also were denied basic rights such as voting until June 2, 1924, when Congress finally granted them citizenship. In the 1960s the African American fight for civil rights inspired Native Americans to start battling the federal government to treat them more fairly. One way they did this was to demand that federal and state governments honor promises they had made in nineteenth-century treaties with Native American tribes. In return for surrendering their land, the treaties had awarded Native Americans hunting and fishing rights in their native homelands. Native Americans had not used them in the past. When they began exercising their rights in the 1960s, many of them were arrested.

On October 13, 1968, Sid Mills, a member of the Puyallup tribe, was arrested for fishing with nets in the Nisqually River in Washington State. "We will fight for our rights,"[41] Mills said. After repeated fishing protests like his, the Puyallup tribe won the fishing rights the treaties had guaranteed them. Other tribes, like the Winnebago in Wisconsin, staged similar protests to win similar fishing rights.

The new Native American militancy erupted a year later in a dramatic incident on Alcatraz, an island off the coast of San Francisco, California, where a famous federal prison once operated. On the morning of November 20, 1969, seventy-nine Native Americans, including married couples and children, began occupying Alcatraz in a protest that drew worldwide attention. Occupiers claimed the land rightfully belonged to Native Americans and wanted to make it a center of their culture. Vine Deloria Jr., a Sioux Indian and noted historian, says the protest made the nation aware of problems facing Native Americans, such as lack of educational opportunities, high unemployment, and racism.

"Alcatraz," Deloria says, "was a big enough symbol that for the first time [in the twentieth century] Indians were taken seriously."[42]

The occupiers held the island until June 11, 1971, when federal officials forcefully removed them. But that protest and others by Native Americans, including the Wounded Knee Occupation, convinced the government to treat Native Americans more equitably. In 1970 and 1971, Congress passed fifty-two legislative proposals to allow Native Americans more power to govern themselves on reservations. The federal government in the 1970s also doubled funds for health care for Native Americans and for money spent on reservations.

At the same time Native Americans were protesting, African Americans also were winning rights that had long been denied them.

Lynching and Race Riots

The first African Americans arrived in the New World in 1619 as indentured servants but within a few decades most blacks arriving in the New World were sold as slaves to anyone who wanted to buy them. Although some blacks managed to gain their freedom, most African Americans lived in slavery until the end of the Civil War in 1865. For the next century after slavery was abolished, whites in many areas of the nation denied blacks basic rights and used violence to make them submissive to white rule. This included denying blacks due process under the law. Whites would often decide on their own that a black person was guilty of a crime and impose a death sentence. Between 1882 and 1968, at least 3,445 African Americans were lynched, almost all of them in southern states. The term *lynch* means to kill someone by any means—including hanging, beating, shooting, or burning—as punishment for some crime, but without giving the person a proper and legal trial.

Even though lynchings were brutal, huge crowds sometimes gathered to watch them. On May 21, 1917, whites seized Ell Persons, a black man accused of slaying a white teenager. The *Memphis Press* later described the mob that gleefully watched his death:

> Fifteen thousand of them—men, women, even little children [cheered] as they poured the gasoline on the fiend and struck the match. They fought and screamed and crowded to get a glimpse of him, and the mob closed in and struggled about the fire as the flames flared high and the smoke rolled about their heads. Two of them hacked off his ears as he burned; another tried to cut off a toe but they stopped him.[43]

Whites sometimes attacked blacks in race riots. On April 13, 1873, in Colfax, Louisiana, 150 blacks were beaten or shot to death in a dispute over which political party had won elections the previous November. The massacre began at the Colfax County Courthouse when whites murdered blacks who had gathered there. Whites then went to black areas of town to beat and kill more African Americans and burn their homes. Historian Eric Foner calls it "the bloodiest single instance of racial carnage in the Reconstruction era."[44] Reconstruction was the period from the end of the Civil War to 1873 when southern blacks briefly enjoyed rights like voting because U.S. troops stationed in the South protected them. When troops left, southern whites took away those rights.

There also were race riots in the early twentieth century after blacks began moving to northern states in large numbers. Black poet James Weldon Johnson nicknamed the summer of 1919 "Red Summer" because there were more than two dozen riots against blacks in cities like Chicago, Illinois; Philadelphia, Pennsylvania; and New York, New York. In Chicago on July 27 Eugene Williams, a black youth, drowned in Lake Michigan after whites threw rocks at him because he was swimming in an area reserved for whites. In the next five days at least twenty-three blacks and fifteen whites were killed in sporadic fighting and about one thousand blacks were left homeless when whites destroyed their homes. According to a 1922 report on the riot:

> many Negroes were attacked by white ruffians. Street-car routes, especially at transfer points, were the centers of lawlessness. Trolleys were pulled from the wires, and Negro passengers were dragged into the street, beaten, stabbed, and shot. Raids into the Negro residence area then began. Automobiles sped

through the streets, the occupants shooting at random. Negroes retaliated by "sniping" [shooting guns] from ambush.[45]

For almost a century after slavery ended, African Americans had to endure such violence and were often denied their civil rights. They finally began to win equality with whites and protection under the law through a series of historic protests that lasted more than a decade.

The Civil Rights Movement

Even though African Americans had been battling for their rights since slavery, in the 1950s they were still discriminated against in every part of the country. Life for blacks was hardest in the South, where they were forced to endure segregated living conditions. Blacks could not enter businesses reserved for whites, and they had to attend separate schools. They also were denied basic rights, like voting. Southern laws even forced blacks to sit in the rear of buses and to surrender their

A group of white children cheer outside an African American residence that they have set on fire in Chicago in 1919. Black poet James Weldon Johnson nicknamed the summer of 1919 "Red Summer" because there were more than two dozen race riots in cities like Chicago.

seat if a white person wanted to sit down. But on December 1, 1955, Rosa Parks, a black woman, refused to give up her seat to a white man on a bus in Montgomery, Alabama. She said later, "We [had] finally reached the point were we [blacks] had to take action."[46] Her personal protest led to her arrest and a year-long boycott of buses by Montgomery blacks which resulted in the U.S. Supreme Court ruling that the Montgomery law was illegal. Similar protests in other southern cities also succeeded in integrating buses so blacks could sit anywhere they wanted.

The pace of protest picked up in the 1960s when blacks battled segregation by staging sit-ins at restaurants that served only whites and by attending white universities. On September 30, 1962, James Meredith became the first black admitted to the University of Mississippi. He won the right to attend the school by filing a lawsuit in federal court claiming his rights were being violated by being refused admission to the school. "My purpose was to break the system of 'White supremacy' at any cost and going to the university was just one of the many steps,"[47] Meredith said. Hundreds of whites came to the campus the day Meredith entered the school to protest his presence. In an armed confrontation with 300 federal marshals who were guarding Meredith, two civilians were shot to death and 166 federal marshals were injured. Meredith was not harmed and later graduated from the university.

Blacks staged scores of massive marches to defeat segregation. One of the most dramatic was on May 12, 1963, when 6,000 people ages six to sixteen marched to the segregated downtown area of Birmingham, Alabama. While they knelt and prayed, police arrested 959 youths for parading without a permit—white officials had refused them permission for the march. When fifteen-year-old Grosbeck Preer Parham appeared in court, a white judge warned him that blacks should quit protesting. The judge advised him that blacks should be patient and they would eventually get their rights. The teenager replied, "We've been waiting over one hundred years."[48]

The protests of the 1960s ended the century of injustice by forcing the federal government to intervene and make southern states end segregation and give blacks their rights. Although the victories made life better for blacks, African Americans have continued to protest into the twenty-first century to achieve true equality with whites.

Besides Native Americans and African Americans another group of Americans also has faced racial discrimination for centuries—Asian Americans.

Asian Discrimination and Protests

The first large wave of Asian immigrants came to the United States in the mid–nineteenth century to work in California gold mines and to build the transcontinental railroad. They often faced racism from whites. In 1871 a white mob descended on Chinatown in Los Angeles, California, destroying businesses and

A crowd gathers for the March on Washington to listen to Martin Luther King Jr. deliver his famous "I Have a Dream Speech." This march is perhaps the most important civil rights protest in history.

homes and killing eighteen Asians. In 1885 whites in Rock Springs, Wyoming, murdered about thirty Chinese workers.

Japanese immigrants faced similar racist attacks. In the 1940s when the United States began fighting Japan in World War II, the U.S. government forcibly interned one-hundred-twenty-thousand Japanese American men, women, and children in ten different camps across the United States. They were imprisoned in the camps because the government believed they might sabotage the U. S. war effort against their former homeland. Minori Yasui, a lawyer in Oregon, refused to report for evacuation to a relocation camp to protest the unjust order. He explains, "[By] god, I had to stand up and say, 'That's wrong.' I refused to report for evacuation. Sure enough, within the week, I got a telephone call from the military police saying, 'We're coming to get

The March on Washington

On August 28, 1963, a quarter million people met near the Lincoln Memorial in Washington, D.C. in perhaps the single most important civil rights protest in history. Many actors, sports stars, and other celebrities attended the March on Washington, and the protest is best remembered for a speech given by Martin Luther King Jr. But two veteran civil rights leaders—Bayard Rustin and Ralph Abernathy—believe the protest's true importance was the impact of so many people gathering together on a single day to support African American civil rights. In the following excerpts, each offers a comment on that day:

Bayard Rustin: It wasn't the Harry Belafontes [a famous singer] and the greats from Hollywood that made the march. What made the march was that black people voted that day with their feet. They came from every state, they came in jalopies, on trains, buses, anything they could get—some walked.

Ralph Abernathy: The March on Washington established visibility in this nation. It showed the struggle [for black rights] was nearing a close, that people were coming together, that all the organizations could stand together. It demonstrated that there was a unity in the black community for the cause of freedom and justice. It made it clear that we did not have to use violence to achieve the goals which we were seeking.

Quoted in Henry and Steve Fayer, *Voices of Freedom: An Oral History of the Civil Rights Movement from the 1950s Through the 1980s*, New York: Bantam, 1990, pp. 169–170.

you.'"[49] He and other Japanese Americans spent three years in the camps.

Racism against Asians eased after World War II but strengthened again in the 1980s when Japanese automakers began selling more cars than U.S. automakers, which resulted in some U.S. workers losing their jobs. On June 19, 1982, Vincent Chin, a Chinese American, was beaten to death with a baseball bat in Detroit, Michigan, by Ronald Ebens and Michael Nitz, who mistakenly believed Chin was Japanese. When Judge Charles Kaufman sentenced the attackers to only three years probation and fines of several thousands dollars, Asian Americans formed the American Citizens for Justice. The group staged protests, demanded a retrial, and asked the federal government to investigate whether Chin's civil rights had been violated. Although Ebens and Nitz were acquitted on federal charges, the incident led to a renewed fight by Asian Americans for just treatment. Two decades later in a ceremony remembering Chin's death, Elaine Akagi, who

Chasing the Chinese from Seattle

During the nineteenth century, there were many incidents in which racist whites attacked and even killed Chinese people. On February 7, 1886, white residents of Seattle, Washington, came up with a somewhat less-violent way to get rid of Chinese residents. An article in *Harper's Weekly* magazine explains,

> By a preconcerted plan, of which neither the law-abiding citizens of the town nor the Chinamen had a hint, a mob invaded the Chinese quarter late Saturday night, forcibly but quietly entered the houses, dragged the occupants from their beds, forced them quickly to pack their personal effects, and marched them to a steamer. The mob was thoughtful enough to provide wagons to convey the baggage of its victims. Some had money enough to pay their fare to San Francisco, and many did not, but the mob made no distinction. The few policemen that became aware of the wrong-doing had no power and slight willingness to prevent it, and before the sleeping citizens of the town or the county officers knew what was going on, 400 Chinamen were shivering on the dock.

> Police and a local militia finally rescued the Chinese but not before a mob of two thousand whites fought the militia, resulting in one death. At least half the Chinese left Seattle anyway because they were frightened whites would harm them.

"Anti-Chinese Riot at Seattle," *Harper's Weekly*, March 6, 1886, p. 155.

helped coordinate the memorial to the slain Chin, said, "As tragic as [his] death was, one good thing was that it banded Asian Americans together. If nothing else, we started working together on issues, not only Vincent's death."[50]

On May 5, 2006, Asian Americans continued to stand up for themselves when they held protests in several cities over a federal law that would make illegal immigrants felons. Asians joined other groups like Mexican Americans in opposing the law because there are tens of thousands Asians and Mexicans in the United States illegally. Although the House of Representatives passed the bill the Senate rejected it, but there have been other attempts in Congress since then to make illegal immigrants felons. As with other protests, it at least made more Americans aware of the concerns Asians have about federal immigration laws.

Another group that shares the concerns Asians have over illegal immigrants are Mexican Americans. They also have been active for a long time in fighting against racism and for civil rights.

Hispanic Protests

The first Mexican Americans lived in California and parts of the Southwest before the United States won that territory from Mexico in the 1840s. Mexican Americans and other Hispanics experienced

Lillian Chin, mother of murder victim Vincent Chin, sobs as she leaves a Detroit court. The two white men found guilty of beating Chin to death were only sentenced to three years probation.

The Zoot Suit Riots

A zoot suit is a high-waisted suit with wide-legged, tight-cuffed trousers and a long coat that has wide lapels and wide padded shoulders. During World War II, zoot suits were popular with Mexican Americans, African Americans, and other minority groups. Riots in the summer of 1943 in Los Angeles, California, between young Latinos and white sailors, soldiers, and civilians were named the zoot suit riots, after the hip clothing. Tensions between the two groups had been high and confrontations were common. On June 3, 1943, some servicemen became angry when they thought some Latinos had threatened them. Later that night the sailors went back and beat up the Latinos. For the next five days, thousands of servicemen and civilians attacked Latinos in the downtown area and in their neighborhoods. The Latinos fought back and defended themselves. The rioting ended June 8 when military authorities prohibited sailors and soldiers from entering the downtown area. Historian George Sanchez explains:

> The way the riots developed is very much attached to what the notion of a zoot-suiter was. The notion of a zoot-suiter was always racialized, even though Mexicans were not the only people wearing zoot suits. So a riot that first was aiming at individuals because of their dress becomes a more expansive sort of riot, aimed at a particular racial population; Mexican-Americans. It didn't take long for the kids from the barrios to organize and fight back.

Quoted in *Zoot Suit Riots*, documentary, directed by Joseph Tovares, PBS, original airdate February 10, 2002, www.pbs.org/wgbh/amex/zoot/eng_filmmore/pt.html.

discrimination from whites in both the nineteenth and twentieth centuries. But by July 1, 2008, there were 46.9 million Hispanics in the United States— 15 percent of the nation's population— and the nation's largest ethnic or racial minority wielded enough political power to protect itself from most harassment and violence from racist whites.

Hispanics, however, were still fighting the twin issues of legal and illegal immigration—they wanted it to be easier for Hispanics to come to the United States and for the nation to treat illegal immigrants with more understanding. To show their economic and political clout, on May 1, 2006, Hispanics staged a Day Without Immigrants in which millions of Hispanics refused to go to school, to work, or to shop at any stores. So many workers participated in the protest that some restaurants and other businesses had to close.

On the Day Without Immigrants an estimated 1.1 million Hispanics marched in more than fifty cities, including four hundred thousand in both Chicago and Los Angeles. In Chicago marchers chanted "today we march, tomorrow we vote"[51] to highlight their political strength. In Los Angeles, where people chanted "si, se puede" (yes, it can be done), one of the marchers was Ricardo Meneses, a Mexican who had lived in the United States for fifteen years. Meneses supported the immigrants. He said, "We all come here to look for work. The only thing we can do now is demonstrate peacefully."[52] The one-day protest was one of the largest in U.S. history.

Chapter Five

The Fight for Gender and Sexual Orientation Equality

September 7, 1968, was the final night of the 1968 Miss America Pageant. On that evening nearly four hundred people gathered outside the convention center in Atlantic City, New Jersey, where the beauty contest was being held. The crowd, assembled by New York Radical Women, a militant women's rights group, was there to protest the pageant. The protesters believed it was sexist because it evaluated women based on a standard of beauty imposed by a male-dominated society. Some carried signs that said, "Welcome to the Cattle Auction," and during the pageant, protesters inside the center dropped a banner over a balcony railing that read, "Women's Liberation." The banner appeared on television, and it was the first time many people in the nation had seen the phrase that symbolized the new movement to give women more rights in their every day lives.

Less than a year later, on the night of June 27, 1969, another protest by a group that also wanted more freedom and equal treatment turned violent. In New York City police raided the Stonewall Inn, an unlicensed bar that called itself a private club for gay men and lesbians. Police at that time regularly raided such bars and harassed gays, sometimes arresting them on made-up charges. But customers at the Stonewall that night resisted arrest. When police started arresting the bar's patrons, a crowd started to gather outside the bar. After shouts of "Gay Power" and "We Want Freedom," the crowd joined the Stonewall customers in fighting police. Outnumbered and fearing for their lives, police retreated from the bar. Deputy Inspector Seymour Pine said, "I had been in combat situations [in war] but there was never any time that I felt more scared than then."[53]

Both incidents, one a protest and one a riot, were heavily publicized and made the nation aware of new efforts to fight discrimination based on gender and sexual orientation. Women wanted equality with men while gays wanted the freedom to love whomever they wanted and to live their lives openly. Vern L. Bullough, author of *Before Stonewall: Activists for Gay and Lesbian Rights in Historical Context*, believes both movements flourished when they did because of the successful fight African Americans were waging in the 1960s for equality with whites. Bullough writes, "These movements followed the leadership of those involved in gaining civil rights for blacks."[54] Women and gays employed some of the same tactics blacks had, from mass protests to legal challenges of laws that discriminated against them.

Fighting for Female Equality

The world's first women's rights convention was held in 1848 in Seneca Falls, New York. More than three hundred women and men met on July 19 and 20 to debate and approve a Declaration of Sentiments and Resolutions. This historic document called for an end to gender discrimination against women and laid out the goals of the women's rights movement, from winning the right to vote to gaining legal equality with men. Patterned after the Declaration of Independence, it states:

> We hold these truths to be self-evident: that all men and women are created equal; that they are endowed by their Creator with certain inalienable rights; that among these are life, liberty, and the pursuit of happiness; that to secure these rights governments are instituted,

deriving their just powers from the consent of the governed.[55]

The declaration listed the ways in which women were not equal to men such as not being allowed to go to college or vote. When women got married, their husbands gained financial control over their money and property, and wives were expected to obey their husbands without question. And if husbands physically punished their wives for not obeying them, law enforcement officials would not prosecute the husband. Seneca Falls was the hometown of Elizabeth Cady

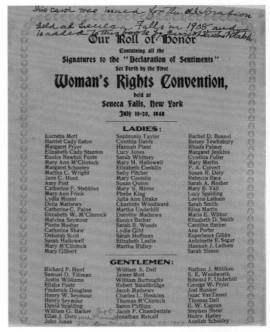

A list of signatures on the Declaration of Sentiments, the document that was debated and approved during the world's first women's rights convention held in 1848 in Seneca Falls, New York. This document called for an end to gender discrimination.

Silent Sentinels

From January 10, 1917, until June 1919, women picketed in front of the White House to protest the federal government's refusal to allow women to vote. The protest ended when Congress approved the Nineteenth Amendment to the U.S. Constitution which gave women the right to vote. The women became known as "Silent Sentinels" because they marched peacefully and quietly while carrying protest signs. Police arrested some of them for obstructing traffic because people in cars stopped to watch them. The following excerpt from an article in *American History* magazine describes the picketing women:

> [Twelve] women carrying banners on long poles took up positions outside the White House gates. In their movement's traditional colors—purple, white and gold—their banners read: "MR. PRESIDENT [Woodrow Wilson], HOW LONG MUST WOMEN WAIT FOR LIBERTY?" They returned every day, in good weather and bad, silently directing this pointed question at the grand house behind them. No one quite knew what to think. Political picketing was uncommon in those days, and unheard of by women. Some passersby gawked, some hurled angry taunts, others were merely amused. The press was sharply divided. The president said nothing. Seemingly unperturbed, he sometimes smiled and tipped his hat at the pickets as his limousine drove through the White House gates. For long grueling weeks the women's severest challenge was a winter so bitingly cold that hands ached and feet felt like blocks of ice.

William Lavender and Mary Lavender, "Suffragists' Storm over Washington," *American History*, October 2003, p. 30.

Stanton, who became a historic leader in the fight for women's rights. She once summed up the plight of women this way: "While man enjoys all the rights, he preaches all the duties to a woman."[56]

Starting with Suffrage

Women realized the key to achieving equality with men was winning the right to vote. This would enable them to elect officials who supported them. The fight for women's suffrage—the right to vote—was their major goal, but it took women seven decades to achieve it. Women and their male supporters held political rallies, signed petitions, and engaged in acts of civil disobedience to win the right to vote. Lucy Stone of Massachusetts refused to pay taxes because she could not vote. To get payment for the taxes she owed, officials seized Stone's household goods, including her baby's cradle.

Two suffragists being arrested during protests outside the White House in 1917. After being put in jail, suffragists were often beaten, treated abusively, and sometimes force-fed while attempting to participate in hunger strikes.

In 1869 Stone started the American Woman Suffrage Association, which became the most influential of several groups working for women's suffrage. In 1890 Wyoming became the first state to grant women the right to vote and eventually other states also began allowing women voters. It was harder to convince the federal government to grant that right because it required a change in the U.S. Constitution. In 1878 a constitutional amendment to allow women to vote was introduced for the first time in the name of women's rights activist Susan B. Anthony. Congress,

however, rejected it repeatedly in the next four decades.

In 1917 Alice Paul created the National Woman's Party (NWP) to force the federal government to allow women voters. On January 10, 1917, a dozen NWP members began picketing the White House to persuade President Woodrow Wilson to support suffrage. On June 22 police arrested two women picketers on a charge of obstructing traffic because cars were stopping to watch them. Police arrested more women in the next few months including Paul on October 20. Many protesters were beaten and treated abusively in jail, and Paul was one of several women brutally force-fed with tubes during a hunger strike to protest their arrest. Paul was freed on November 27. She was so weak she could hardly stand but she defiantly told reporters, "We were put out of jail as we were put in—at the whim of the government."[57]

The bravery of the women protesters convinced Wilson to finally support their right to vote on January 9, 1918. But the women protesters, known as Silent Sentinels, continued picketing daily until June when Congress approved the Nineteenth Amendment to the Constitution to allow women to vote. The amendment was ratified by the states on August 18, 1920. Passage of the Nineteenth Amendment, however, did not end the fight for equal rights with men.

Women's Liberation

Women made progress in many areas in the decades after they won the right to vote. They could attend college, engage

Women's Liberation and Lesbians

The women's liberation movement was supported by many individual groups around the country. One of them was the Chicago Women's Liberation Union (CWLU), which worked to support women's causes from 1969 to 1977. Although lesbians experienced the same problems all women did, some leaders of the national women's liberation movement like Betty Friedan discouraged lesbian members because they feared being associated with lesbians would hurt the movement's reputation. But in an Internet history of the CWLU, Elaine Wessel states that the Chicago group welcomed lesbians. In the following excerpt, Wessel writes about the close connection between the gay and women's liberation movements:

Lesbian organizing began in the CWLU somewhat informally before evolving into a work group called the Gay Group. The Gay Group was reorganized into the Lesbian Group, which was usually called "Blazing Star" from the name of the very successful newsletter it produced. Beginning very early in CWLU's history, there were lesbian groupings within the organization, and connections between CWLU lesbian members and other organizations in Chicago's lesbian and gay communities. The modern gay liberation movement (which began with the Stonewall riots against the New York police in June 1969) began almost simultaneously with the women's liberation movement, of which CWLU was a part.

Elaine Wessel, "Blazing Star," Chicago Women's Liberation Union, www.cwluherstory.org/blazing-star.html.

in political activity, and were more readily accepted in jobs previously denied them, such as with the military and in police and fire departments. However, in the 1960s women were still not treated equally in many areas including the workplace, where they were still denied certain jobs and paid less than men. Women in that decade became more forceful in demanding equality. Their fight became known as the women's liberation movement, and its goal was to achieve legal and social equality with men. The movement provided many new opportunities for women in the workplace, sports, and in politics, as female candidates were elected to many levels of government. However, repeated attempts by women's groups to pass an Equal Rights Amendment to the U.S. Constitution that would bar any discrimination based on sexual gender has failed for decades. The amendment was originally introduced in 1923 and has been unsuccessfully re-introduced in every session of Congress since then including on July 21, 2009, by Representative Carolyn B. Maloney, a New York Democrat. Thus women have never won one of their biggest battles for equality.

The Bitter Battle over Abortion

Women also have waged a bitter fight over abortion for more than four decades. In the 1960s many states restricted the right of women to have an abortion, which forced thousands of women to get abortions illegally. Many women believed they should have complete control over their own body, and they began working to repeal laws limiting abortion by challenging the laws in court. On January 22, 1973, in the *Roe v. Wade* court case, the U.S. Supreme Court overturned a Texas law restricting abortion and said women could terminate their pregnancy in the first six months. The ruling legalized abortion throughout the United States. The outcome of *Roe v. Wade* was considered a major triumph for women's rights, but people who opposed abortion immediately began fighting to once again criminalize abortion. This fierce battle has played a major role in national politics ever since.

Pro-choice activists continue to engage in many protests to publicize the issue. One of the most massive was the April 24, 2004, March for Women's Lives when between 500,000 and 1.1 million people—crowd estimates of the march vary widely—held a rally in Washington, D.C. Hillary Rodham Clinton, a New York senator at the time and a speaker at the rally, drew cheers when she told the protesters she had attended a similar 1992 women's march. Clinton also said, "We elected a pro-choice president [her husband, Bill Clinton, in 1992]. This year we've got to do it again."[58] Clinton urged people to help elect Democratic senator John Kerry in the presidential campaign that year, but the pro-choice candidate lost to Republican George W. Bush, who opposes abortion and was reelected to a second term.

The election was close and some of those votes against Kerry were cast by

Pro-choice activists gathered in large numbers during the 2004 March for Women's Lives rally in Washington, D.C. During the rally New York Senator Hillary Rodham Clinton urged the crowd to elect the pro-choice candidate for president, Democratic Senator John Kerry.

anti-abortion supporters. They also have engaged in dramatic protests to publicize their political point of view. One tactic they have used is to picket outside medical offices where abortions are performed to scare pregnant women away. An annual Life Chain protest held every October has seen hundreds of thousands of pro-life protesters lining city streets or long stretches of highway while carrying signs that attack abortion or display images of dead fetuses. The first such protest was held in 1987 in Marysville, California, by 250 sign-carrying protesters and since then has spread to every state. LifeChain.Net, a Web site that coordinates the protests,

says, "Life Chain is a peaceful and prayerful public witness of pro-life Americans standing for one hour praying for our nation and for an end to abortion."[59]

Most people who oppose abortion do so because of religious beliefs. Many of those same people also disagree with the way gays and lesbians live.

Gay Pride

Gays and lesbians were tolerated in some societies in the past, such as ancient Greece and Rome. For centuries, however, they have been discriminated against because society in general considers their sexual orientation abnormal.

As late as the 1960s, many states still had laws that prohibited sexual contact between members of the same sex. Even though such laws were rarely enforced, police often harassed gays and lesbians by arresting them for minor violations of the law or on made-up charges.

On January 1, 1967, police beat and arrested more than a dozen people at the Black Cat Bar in Los Angeles, California, for kissing each other because they were of the same sex. They were kissing to celebrate the new year, a traditional way for many people to greet the new year, but because the partygoers were gay, the traditional gesture was technically illegal. The arrests touched off protests in which gays and lesbians marched carrying signs that read, "NO MORE ABUSE OF OUR RIGHTS AND DIGNITY" and "BLUE [police] FASCISM MUST GO!" An editorial in the *Advocate*, a gay newspaper, predicted that gays and lesbians would no longer passively allow police or anyone else to deny them their rights. The newspaper boldly declared, "We do not ask for our rights on bended knee. We demand them, standing tall, as dignified human beings. We will not go away."[60]

ACT UP

Acquired immunodeficiency syndrome (AIDS) became a worldwide epidemic in the early 1980s. At the time governmental officials were slow to fund research and treatment of AIDS because of their prejudice against gay men, a group that was hit hard by the disease. In March 1987 the AIDS Coalition to Unleash Power (ACT UP) was created at the Lesbian and Gay Community Services Center in New York City to protest the lack of concern over AIDS. ACT UP staged many dramatic protests to attract media coverage about the need for more funding. On September 14, 1989, seven ACT UP members invaded the New York Stock Exchange and chained themselves to a balcony to protest the high price of AIDS drugs. A protest by forty-five hundred people at New York's St. Patrick's Cathedral in December 1989 was one of many at churches which condemned homosexuality. One of the most daring protests came on January 22, 1991, when three ACT UP members entered the studio of the CBS Evening News at the beginning of the nationally televised broadcast. Anchorman Dan Rather had just introduced himself when the ACT UP members shouted "Fight AIDS not Arabs! Fight AIDS not Arabs." Microphones picked up the protesters' voices which prompted Rather to cut immediately to a commercial so the audience would not hear more of the protest.

A New Openness

The prophecy declared by the *Advocate* in 1967 came true with the riot at the Stonewall Inn in New York in 1969. That riot is considered a historic turning point in the fight by gays and lesbians for their rights. The fact that the customers of Stonewall Inn openly fought police helped bring the plight of gays and lesbians to the attention of the public and emboldened many gays and lesbians elsewhere to stand up for their rights. Gays and lesbians often kept their sexual orientation secret from family, friends, and coworkers for fear of being shunned or discriminated against. But the gay rights movement in the 1960s led many more gays and lesbians to let their sexual orientation be known.

The gay rights movement of the 1960s allowed more gays and lesbians to make their sexual orientation public. As a result, an estimated one hundred thousand people participated in the National March on Washington for Lesbian and Gay Rights on October 14, 1979.

This new openness allowed an estimated one hundred thousand people to conduct the National March on Washington for Lesbian and Gay Rights on October 14, 1979. Lesbian photographer and filmmaker Joan E. Biren commented a quarter century later on the effect of that highly visible protest. She said:

> You were just amazed and astounded to see so many of our own people in one place. I was very publicly out, but there were not too many others who were. The triumph of the 1979 march was that so many people did come out. To me, the importance was we were going to be a political force. This was the most visible we had ever been.[61]

The mass gathering was similar to smaller Gay Pride parades or festivals already being held throughout the nation to create awareness of the struggle by gays and lesbians for their rights. Another march in the nation's capital on October 12, 1987, drew twice as many people. The fact that two openly gay members of Congress—Massachusetts representatives Gerry E. Studds and Barney Frank—spoke to the crowd showed how far gays had come in their fight for equality and acceptance by other Americans. That battle, however, has still not ended.

In the four decades after Stonewall, the fight for gay rights has come to include bisexuals and transgender people who also are discriminated against because of their sexual orientation. The LGBT (lesbian, gay, bisexual, and transgender) community has won legal protections against job discrimination, state and federal hate crime laws that protect them from people who harm them because of their lifestyle, and the repeal of laws that criminalize same-gender sex. Through protests and political action, the LGBT community also has won more funding for research and treatment of acquired immunodeficiency syndrome (AIDS), a sexually transmitted disease that appeared in 1981 and heavily affected members of the gay, lesbian, bisexual, and transgender community.

Despite those victories, gays and lesbians in the twenty-first century still were battling for two major rights—to be able to serve openly in the U.S. armed forces and to legally marry.

Gays in the Military

The U.S. military officially bans gays and lesbians from serving in any of the armed forces. There are gays and lesbians in the military, however, and they are there because they keep their sexual orientation a secret. If their sexual orientation is discovered, they often are treated brutally by other soldiers and dishonorably discharged. In 1993 when gays and lesbians demanded greater acceptance in the military, President Bill Clinton initiated a "Don't Ask, Don't Tell" policy in which military officials could not ask service members if they were gay or lesbian and service members were not to "tell," or reveal, their sexual orientation. But the military still officially banned gays and lesbians and in the first fifteen years the "Don't Ask, Don't Tell" policy was in effect, the military discharged more than twelve thousand gay and lesbian service members when their superiors learned their sexual orientation.

In September 2008 the air force discharged Lieutenant Colonel Victor Fehrenbach because he is gay. Fehrenback is an eighteen-year veteran who had flown combat missions in Iraq and Afghanistan. He claimed being gay did not interfere with doing his duty, and he was crushed he had to leave the service. "The Air Force has been my life," he said. "I was born on an Air Force base [his parents were in the service]. I was faced with the end of my life as I knew it."[62]

Fehrenbach's life-long connection to the military ended when he lost an appeal to stay in the Air Force. Aubrey Sarvis is executive director of the Servicemembers Legal Defense Network, a nonprofit group dedicated to lifting the military ban on gays and lesbians. He believes Bill Clinton's policy was wrong. He says, "I see very few, if any, good things about 'Don't Ask, Don't Tell.' It means you have to lie or deceive every day."[63]

Same-Sex Marriage

Another battle gays and lesbians still were fighting in the twenty-first century was to be able to legally marry their

A gay couple getting married on the steps of the Polk County Administration Building in Des Moines, Iowa. In 2009 Iowa become one of a half-dozen states that legally allowed same-sex marriages to take place.

same-sex partners. Gay and lesbian couples wanted to show their love for each other by marrying like heterosexual couples. They also wanted the legal rights married couples have, such as spousal workplace benefits and being able to jointly own property. By 2009 a half dozen states, including Massachusetts, Connecticut, and Iowa, had changed their laws to allow gay and lesbian couples to marry. Even more states had approved spousal rights for gays and lesbians who lived together as a couple. The federal government, however, does not recognize same-sex marriages because of the 1996 Defense of Marriage law which defines marriage as a union between one man and one woman.

There have been thousands of marches, rallies, and other protests by both sides in the battle over same-sex marriage. On August 16, 2009, a Nationwide Kiss-In was held in Washington, D.C.; San Francisco; Atlanta; Salt Lake City; and dozens of other cities. Gay and lesbian couples were joined by heterosexual couples to show that people have a right to show their love for each other, even to marry each other, no matter what their sexual orientation. The Salt Lake City kiss-in drew a lot of media attention because the Mormon church, which is headquartered there, opposes gay marriage and claims gay and lesbian sex is a sin. Kate Savage, a Brigham Young University graduate who attended the kiss-in with her boyfriend, Tristan Call, criticizes the church for its stance. She says, "It's as if the doctrine of the importance of families we're taught is used to destroy other people's families, and we don't understand that."[64]

Making History

Women who have fought for their rights have often had to do things that outraged other people, such as picketing the White House to gain the right to vote. By doing so, they made history. Historian Laurel Thatcher Ulrich writes, "Well-behaved women seldom make history."[65] Ulrich's comment also can be applied to gays, lesbians, and every other person who has taken a stand on a controversial issue that mattered to them.

Chapter Six

Opposing War

At least some Americans have opposed every war in which the United States has fought, including the American Revolution. John Adams, the second U.S. president, claimed that during the American Revolution, at least one-third of colonists opposed the war. Opponents included people sympathetic to ongoing British rule and members of religious groups like the Quakers who opposed all wars. Stephen Howell, a Quaker, was jailed for three months in 1778 for failing to pay a fine after he refused to join the colonial army. The April minutes of the New Garden Monthly Meeting of Friends noted that when their fellow Quaker was jailed, "he felt such sweetness of mind as encouraged him to persevere on in suffering for the testimony of a good conscience [for not fighting]."[66] Colonists who supported the war often treated opponents brutally, sometimes tarring and feathering them.

The United States needed so many soldiers during the Civil War that for the first time it had to draft civilians to fight. In July 1863 when the government began naming men who it would draft, so many violent protests occurred that the *Washington Times* newspaper wrote, "The nation is at this time in a state of Revolution, North, South, East, and West."[67] The worst violence occurred in New York City where rioters damaged draft offices, public buildings, and the homes of city officials and Republican party leaders.

During the Vietnam War in the 1960s and 1970s, tens of millions of people protested the nation's involvement in the conflict. Historian Howard Zinn claims more Americans opposed that war than any other. Zinn writes, "This was the greatest movement against war in the nation's history. On October 15, 1969, perhaps two million people across the nation gathered not only in the big cities, but in towns and villages that had never seen an anti-war demonstration."[68]

The Moratorium to End the War in Vietnam on October 15 was the largest antiwar protest in U.S. history. Protesters that day were doing what Americans had for nearly two centuries—opposing their nation's involvement in a war.

Opposing the Draft

The issue of slavery literally divided the nation, resulting in the Civil War. The fierce fighting killed and wounded so many men that President Abraham Lincoln was forced to sign the Conscription Act on March 3, 1863, to draft men into military service. A draft forces civilians into military service. However, men who were drafted could hire a substitute to replace them or purchase an exemption for $300. Some people opposed the draft because they believed it was unfair to allow rich people to buy their way out of the war or because they did not think the government had the right to force anyone to join the army.

In New York from July 13 to July 16, rioters killed 120 people and caused extensive damage before five regiments of soldiers ended the violence. Because the war was being fought over slavery, rioters targeted blacks, setting fire to the

The burning of the Colored Orphan Asylum during the Civil War Draft Riot in New York in 1863. Rioters were protesting being drafted into military service during the Civil War as well as other issues related to the war.

Colored Orphan Asylum and brutally murdering at least a dozen African Americans. Rioters scared so many blacks out of New York that historian Iver Bernstein claims, "For months after the riots the public life of the city became a more noticeably white domain."[69]

When the United States entered World War I in 1917, so many Americans were against the idea of joining the war that the government once again had to draft soldiers. Georgia senator Thomas Hardwick said, "There was undoubtedly general and widespread opposition on the part of many thousands to the enactment of the draft [and] mass meetings in every part of the States protested against it."[70] Even though the federal government passed a law making it illegal to oppose the war, about 900 people were jailed for speaking against conflict. In addition, more than 330,000 men avoided the draft so they would not have to go to war. In Oklahoma 450 members of the Socialist Party and International Workers of the World labor union were jailed for planning a march to the nation's capital to protest the draft. Sentences for the men ranged from sixty days in jail to ten years for the leaders of the planned protest.

The Japanese attack on Pearl Harbor in Hawaii on December 7, 1941, made most Americans eager to fight in World War II. Although ten million men were drafted, only forty-three thousand refused to fight in the war. Six thousand men were imprisoned for refusing to join the armed forces, including David Dellinger, who was studying to be a minister. In October 1943 Dellinger and seven other students were sentenced to three years in prison for refusing to register for the draft. Dellinger was surprised that the criminals the students met in prison accepted them. He said, "They were friendly to us while saying to me such things as 'I am in jail for killing people but you are here for refusing to kill anyone. It doesn't make sense.'"[71]

War never made sense to Dellinger. Four decades later Dellinger would again oppose another conflict the United States was engaged in—the Vietnam War.

Vietnam War Inspires New Levels of Protest

The Vietnam War was a military conflict fought from 1959 to April 30, 1975, between Communist North Vietnam and democratic South Vietnam for control of both nations. In the late 1950s the United States, as part of its global battle against communism, began sending military advisers to South Vietnam to train its army to fight North Vietnam. In 1964 President Lyndon B. Johnson began sending more soldiers to help South Vietnam fight because it was losing the war. When Johnson boosted the number of soldiers there from twenty-three thousand in 1965 to eight hundred twenty thousand by 1968, he ignited the fiercest antiwar opposition the United States had ever seen. It also was the most creative, as protesters invented new ways to oppose war.

Many people once again protested the draft. When men turned eighteen, they were required by law to register for the draft with the Selective Service System.

Although boxer Muhammad Ali was stripped of his title for refusing to serve in the military during the Vietnam War, he did not have to go to jail like so many others who refused to be drafted.

They then received draft cards which they were supposed to carry at all times. At antiwar rallies, young men set their draft cards on fire, holding them high as a symbol of resistance. Many men were arrested for doing that. Some men protested by refusing to register for the draft or for refusing to report for the medical examination to see if they were physically fit to be drafted. On May 2, 1968, Philip Supina wrote to his draft board in Tucson, Arizona, and said he would not take a physical because "I have absolutely no intention [of aiding] in any way the American war effort against the people of Vietnam."[72]

When men who were drafted refused to report for service, they were jailed. The most famous person to refuse to report for service was heavyweight-boxing champion Muhammad Ali. On April 28, 1967, he refused to be inducted into the army. Ali was a Muslim who opposed the war for religious reasons. But like many blacks, he also was reluctant to fight a war so South Vietnamese people could have democratic rights that African Americans in the United States still did not have. Ali said, "I ain't got no quarrel with them Viet Cong [Communist fighters]. They never called me nigger."[73]

Boxing officials quickly stripped Ali of his title for refusing to join the army, and he was found guilty on June 20, 1967, of the felony charge of refusing induction. Ali appealed the conviction and the U.S. Supreme Court overturned it in 1971, which means he did not go to prison. However, many of the more than

ninety-one hundred people who refused to be drafted did spend time in prison. In addition, as many as one hundred thousand men fled the country to avoid fighting or being jailed.

There also were several incidents in which antiwar groups broke into government offices and destroyed draft records. On May 17, 1968, nine people who became known as the Catonsville Nine took 378 draft files from a government office in Catonsville, Maryland, and set them on fire in a parking lot with homemade napalm. One of the burglars was Daniel Berrigan, a Jesuit priest.

Opposition to the war even spread to soldiers. It is estimated that during the Vietnam War, fifty thousand to one hundred thousand soldiers deserted the military, usually by fleeing to another country. Others refused to go to Vietnam when ordered to report there. On June 30, 1966, army privates James Johnson, David Samas, and Dennis Mora decided not to go to Vietnam when they got their orders. They were nicknamed the Fort Hood Three because they were based at Fort Hood army base in Texas. In a statement, the soldiers said, "We have made our decision. We will not be a part of this unjust, immoral, and illegal war. We want no part of a war of extermination. We oppose the criminal waste of American lives and resources. We refuse to go to Vietnam!!"[74]

The Fort Hood Three were court-martialed and sentenced to several years in prison. Many soldiers who fought in Vietnam became convinced the war was wrong, and after their tour of duty was

A Violent Convention

The 1968 Democratic National Convention in Chicago, Illinois, was marred by antiwar protests that raged outside the convention center where delegates nominated Hubert H. Humphrey to run for president. The ten thousand demonstrators demanding an end to the war were outnumbered by twelve thousand police officers, six thousand National Guard members, and six thousand army troops. The chanting, marching protesters clashed repeatedly with police and soldiers who beat them with clubs and used tear gas to

Demonstrators protesting the Vietnam War face off with National Guardsmen during the 1968 Democratic National Convention in Chicago. A report released later that year stated that police provoked the protesters and were unnecessarily brutal to them.

disperse them and keep them from camping in Grant Park. The Walker Report, a federal government study of the violence during the convention released December 1, 1968, said police provoked protesters and were unnecessarily brutal in what it claimed was a "police riot." Fred Turner, who worked for the CBS television network, was on the scene. In the following excerpt, he describes how police were treating protesters:

> Now they're moving in, the cops are moving and they are really belting these characters. They're grabbing them, sticks are flailing. People are laying on the ground. I can see them [cops] are just belting them; cops are just laying it in. There's piles of bodies on the street. There's no question about it. You can hear the screams, and there's a guy they're just dragging along the street and they don't care. I don't think—I don't know if he's alive or dead. Holy Jesus, look at him. Five of them are belting him, really, oh, this man will never get up.

Ina Jaffe, "1968 Chicago Riot Left Mark on Political Protests," NPR, August 23, 2008, www.npr.org/templates/story/story.php?storyId=93898277.

complete, they came home and started Vietnam Veterans Against the War (VVAW), a group dedicated to ending the conflict. One member was John Kerry, who in 1968 and 1969 commanded a swift boat that patrolled South Vietnamese rivers. On April 22, 1971, Kerry was the first Vietnam veteran to testify before Congress on proposals to end the war. In a protest the next day, Kerry and hundreds of other veterans symbolically returned their combat decorations to the government by throwing them onto the steps of the Capitol. "There is no violent reason for this," Kerry said. "I'm doing this for peace and justice and to try to help this country wake up once and for all."[75] Kerry's antiwar stance became controversial when he unsuccessfully ran for president in 2004.

In Vietnam Buddhist monks burned themselves to death to protest a war they believed was hurting their nation. On November 2, 1965, Norman Morrison, a Quaker from Baltimore, Maryland, copied them when he doused himself in kerosene in Washington, D.C., and set himself on fire. Morrison was the first of several Americans who used this extreme form of protest against the war. In addition to these individual acts, the Vietnam War led to the largest and most violent antiwar protests in U.S. history.

Mass Protests and Violence

As the number of U.S. soldiers fighting in Vietnam increased, so did the number of people opposing the war. In the summer of 1965 only a few hundred people marched in Washington, D.C. against the war but on October 15, 1969, during the nationwide Moratorium to End the War in Vietnam, two hundred fifty thousand gathered to demand an end to the war. Antiwar rallies and marches were held periodically during the war in every major city and on nearly every college campus.

College students were a major force in antiwar demonstrations, which sometimes turned violent as students fought with police. The University of Wisconsin was one of the most militant antiwar schools, and students clashed repeatedly with police, who used tear gas and physical force to break up the protests. Student Karleton Armstrong remembers how he had to drag an injured friend away from a 1967 protest after police had beaten him. "All the cops went to the hospital," Armstrong said. "All the students who were clubbed took care of themselves."[76] Three years later on August 24, 1970, Armstrong and three other students—his brother Dwight Armstrong, David Fine, and Leo Burt—participated in one of the era's most violent antiwar acts. They exploded a bomb to destroy a research facility the army maintained on campus at Sterling Hall. The bomb did not harm their intended target, but it damaged twenty-six buildings, killed physicist Robert Fassnacht, and injured four other people. The bombers fled and went into hiding but eventually Armstrong and Fine were captured and served prison sentences.

The bombing occurred during the war's most intense period of student protest. During the 1969–1970 academic year, the federal government reported

National Guardsmen wearing gas masks fire tear gas into a crowd of demonstrators protesting the Vietnam War on the campus of Kent State on May 4, 1970. When the gas cleared, four people were dead and nine others were injured.

1,785 student demonstrations, during which students entered and occupied 313 buildings. The most tragic protest was on May 4, 1970, at Kent State in Ohio. When National Guardsmen felt threatened while trying break up an on-campus protest by several thousand students, they fired into the massed group of students, killing four of them and wounding nine others. Douglas Wrentmore, a twenty-year-old sophomore who was shot in the leg, explains:

> The guardsmen, about 50 to 75 of them, had just had a confrontation with the students in the practice football field, and they were marching away. All of a sudden I heard a volley of shots. Girls started screaming. I saw people fall, and I started running and then I fell. I didn't feel anything. One minute I could run and then I could not. Then I saw blood coming from my leg.[77]

Student protests in the next few weeks over the deaths of Allison Krause, Jeffrey Miller, Sandra Scheuer, and William Knox Schroeder were so powerful that they shut down more than four hundred campuses in the first and only nation-wide strike by U.S. students. More than

The Largest Antiwar Protest Ever

On February 15, 2003, more than ten million people in six hundred cities in sixty countries around the world protested the decision by President George W. Bush to invade Iraq. The event, which was the largest antiwar demonstration in history, included an estimated five hundred thousand people in New York City and two million in London, England, the site of the single largest protest. Countries that hosted such demonstrations included Italy, Spain, Germany, Canada, Australia, South Africa, India, Russia, South Korea, and Japan. Even McMurdo Station in Antarctica participated. Despite the gigantic global protest, Bush and allied nations went ahead and began the Iraq War a month later. In a *New York Times* newspaper article printed two days after the protest, reporter Patrick E. Tyler claims the historic protest showed how powerful world opinion can be. Tyler writes:

> The fracturing of the Western alliance over Iraq and the huge antiwar demonstrations around the world this weekend are reminders that there may still be two superpowers on the planet: the United States and world public opinion. In his campaign to disarm Iraq, by war if necessary, President Bush appears to be eyeball to eyeball with a tenacious new adversary: millions of people who flooded the streets of New York and dozens of other world cities to say they are against war based on the evidence at hand.

Patrick E. Tyler, "A New Power in the Streets," *New York Times*, February 17, 2003.

4 million students participated in the protests, some of which were violent and included takeovers of hundreds of school buildings. The protests forced most schools to end the spring semester early and skip final examinations.

The massive opposition by its citizens to the Vietnam War eventually forced the United States to withdraw in defeat from the conflict. The last U.S. soldiers left on April 30, 1975, the day after South Vietnam surrendered. It would be more than a quarter century before the nation would again experience such intense antiwar sentiment.

The Iraq War

On September 11, 2001, terrorists hijacked four passenger airliners and crashed them into the World Trade Center in New York, the Pentagon in Virginia, and a field in Pennsylvania. Nearly three thousand people were killed. The United States believed that Osama bin Laden, the leader of the terrorist group al Qaeda, was responsible for organizing the attack. Because Afghanistan was sheltering bin Laden, the United States and several allies invaded it on October 7, 2001. Although there were some protests, most Americans supported the war. But in 2002 when President George W. Bush said he wanted to invade neighboring Iraq, many more people began protesting in both the United States and other countries. Bush claimed war was justified because Iraq's dictator, Saddam Hussein, was dangerous. The United States believed Iraq had weapons of mass destruction, maybe even an atomic bomb, and that it had supported al Qaeda. Despite protests by people in the United States and around the world, U.S. forces and their allies invaded Iraq on March 20, 2003.

A Gallup poll conducted during the first few days of the war showed that only 5 percent of Americans had protested or publicly opposed the war. But as the fighting dragged on and Bush's justifications for invading Iraq proved false, opposition to the war grew rapidly. There were hundreds of mass protests both for and against the war as well as many individual

Cindy Sheehan protested the Iraq War by camping near President George W. Bush's Crawford, Texas ranch. She also erected crosses to symbolize each soldier killed during the war, one being her son Casey Sheehan.

acts of protest like that of Cindy Sheehan, whose son Casey was killed while fighting on April 4, 2004. In August 2005 Sheehan began camping near President Bush's Texas ranch in a protest of the Iraq War that drew global media coverage. Sheehan explains, "My son enlisted in the army to protect America and give something back to our country. He didn't enlist to be used and misled by a reckless Commander-in-chief [Bush] who sent his troops to preemptively attack and occupy a country that was no imminent threat (or any threat) to our country."[78]

As happened during the Vietnam War, soldiers deserted or refused to fight. Camilo Mejia, a sergeant in the Florida National Guard, served six months in Iraq. But after a two-week furlough at home, Mejia refused to return to duty in March 2004 because he had come to believe that the war was wrong. Mejia was charged with desertion and sentenced to one year in military prison. When Mejia was released from prison on February 15, 2005, he said, "I was a coward not for leaving the war but for being part of it in the first place."[79]

President Bush was narrowly reelected in 2004. In 2008 Illinois Democratic senator Barack Obama was elected president partly because of his opposition to the war. But even though Obama set a timetable for pulling troops out of Iraq, some

Antiwar Protests and the Internet

Act Now to Stop War and End Racism (ANSWER), which was organized after the September 11, 2001, terrorist attacks on the United States, has helped conduct many of the largest protests against the Iraq War. It uses the Internet extensively to alert people to such events by sending e-mails, some of which include PDF attachments that explain the event and suggest what people can do to help make the protest successful. ANSWER employed the instant communication abilities of the Internet to attract one hundred thousand people to a rally at the Vietnam Memorial in Washington, D.C., on October 26, 2002, as well as for many smaller events. Brian Becker, an ANSWER spokesman, explains how easy the Internet makes it to communicate with people to stage a protest: "I've been doing this since the Vietnam War, and even 10 years ago, to get people to be on the same page meant you had to ship out thousands of leaflets, frequently to different cities. Now we can put a leaflet up as a PDF file. People take it down and make their own copies."

Quoted in Eric J.S. Townsend, "E-Activism Connects Protest Groups, Web Makes It Easy to Organize Rallies Quickly," *Hartford Courant*, December 4, 2002.

people believed he was not doing it fast enough. To mark the sixth anniversary of the start of the Iraq War, thousands of people protested on March 21, 2009, in Washington, D.C.; San Francisco; and other cities. Pat Halle of Baltimore, Maryland, voted for Obama but marched in Washington because "We think it's especially important for this new administration to feel the pressure from people that we don't want more war."[80]

Free to Protest

During the Iraq War, millions of Americans protested for and against the conflict. Jeffrey Peskoff, a former army mechanic who served a year in Iraq, supported the war. But he said he was glad antiwar protesters were speaking out because it showed Americans are free to protest their government. "That's Americana in action,"[81] Peskoff said.

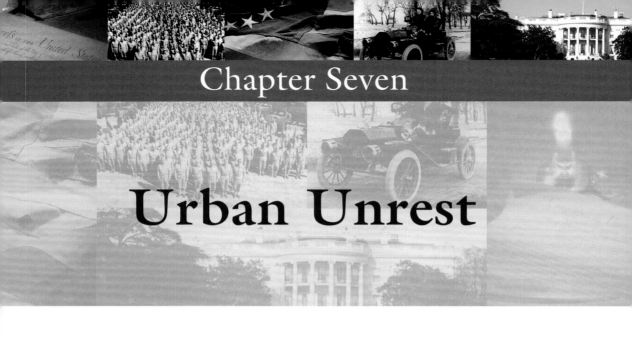

Chapter Seven

Urban Unrest

Most of the major riots and violent disturbances throughout U.S. history have occurred in cities. Historian Richard C. Wade writes, "Violence is no stranger to American cities. [For] two centuries, American cities have known the physical clash of groups, widescale breakdown of established authority, and bloody disorder."[82] It is natural that so much disorder and violence has occurred in cities because in cities many different types of people live in close proximity to one another. This closeness has often allowed differences between various groups of race, nationality, language, or religion to erupt into violence.

Many of the clashes, especially early in the nation's history, involved immigrants who were initially rejected because of such differences. Other urban disorder has ranged from the Stamp Act riots in Boston in 1765 to the riot that erupted in Los Angeles on June 14, 2009,

when the Lakers won the National Basketball Association (NBA) championship. The 1765 disorder was politically motivated and is historic because it marked a major step toward the decision by colonists to fight Great Britain for their freedom in the American Revolution. The Lakers riot, on the other hand, is one of those senseless outbreaks of violence that have sometimes erupted in urban settings for no good reason.

Many urban riots also have started because poor people were angry they had so little compared to other people or believed the government and those who wielded economic and political power were responsible for their plight. This dissatisfaction has led people to react violently throughout U.S. history.

Poor and Food Riots

During the winter months of 1734, poor people in Exeter, New Hampshire, illegally chopped down trees rich people owned so they could burn the wood to keep warm. When British officials sent Daniel Dunbar and a group of armed men to Exeter on April 23 to arrest the thieves, local citizens banded together to stop them. In a report on the incident, an official wrote, "A great number of ill disposed persons assembled themselves [and] in a riotous, tumultuous and most violent manner did beat wound and terribly abuse a number of men hired and [employed] by the Honorable David Dunbar, Esq."[83] Exeter residents fought back because they were sympathetic to the plight of people who only wanted to keep from freezing in the winter cold.

Hunger and not firewood caused the flour riot in New York City on February 10, 1837. When flour merchants hoarded flour to force the price to rise, angry citizens broke into warehouses where the flour was stored and stole it. There also was a riot over bread in Savannah, Georgia, in 1864, when fighting during the Civil War caused food shortages and boosted the prices of food. On April 17, a group of between fifty and one hundred women descended on local stores demanding that the owners sell them bread at a fair price. When the owners did not respond fast enough, the women took it. Three women were arrested but the *News*, the local newspaper, said officials did not want to punish people who were hungry and could not afford to buy food. The article also said, "That the present high prices of provisions have provided distress no one can doubt, and it is probably that some who participated in the riotous proceedings of yesterday were goaded to their course by pressure of want."[84]

The anger people felt over their poverty and the jealousy they harbored toward the rich has caused some riots. Many of those poor were immigrants, who were themselves targets of riots by people who hated the newcomers.

Riots Against Immigrants

When waves of immigrants began arriving in large numbers at various times in the nation's history, some Americans viewed them with hostility and intolerance because of differences in their religions, cultures, and languages. This negative attitude toward immigrants has often led to discrimination that made it difficult for them to get jobs or live where they wanted. According to historian Ralph W. Conant, such discrimination often led to physical confrontations and riots between immigrants and Americans who rejected them. Conant says, "Violent social conflict in America has generally occurred when the established order resisted efforts of new or excluded groups to gain access to rights and opportunities ostensibly available to [everyone]."[85]

Sometimes Americans tried to keep immigrants powerless by preventing them from voting so they could not gain any political power. In 1855 in Louisville, Kentucky, some people were worried that the growing number of German immigrants would influence

RIOT AT HOBOKEN.

In 1851 a riot broke out in New Jersey when German immigrants were attacked by local residents. At various times in the nation's history, some Americans viewed immigrants with hostility and intolerance leading to discrimination.

the August 6 election. The Know-Nothings, a political party that opposed immigrants and Catholics, decided to stop Germans from voting. Know-Nothings gathered at voting locations and beat and even killed German immigrants trying to cast a ballot. When the Germans defended themselves, a gun battle and riot began. Although most historians claim twenty-two

people died in what became known as Bloody Monday, some estimates of the dead range as high as one hundred.

On February 21, 1909, in Omaha, Nebraska, nine hundred men gathered to discuss an incident that occurred two days earlier in which a Greek immigrant shot and killed a police officer who tried to arrest him. At the gathering, attorney H.C. Murphy claimed Greeks were undesirable neighbors. He then called for violence against them. He said, "The blood of an American is on the hands of those Greeks and some method should be adopted to avenge his death and rid the city of this class of persons."[86] The men then rushed into the street toward Greek Town, collecting more participants along the way before they began rioting. Eventually more than three

Rioters looting a pawn shop and carrying off merchandise during the Watts Riots in Los Angeles in August 1965.

thousand men and boys wrecked thirty buildings and burned and looted businesses and homes in Greek Town, where Greek immigrants lived. The mob beat men, women, and children, and one boy died.

Most cities had separate parts of town, like Greek Town, where various ethnic groups lived. They were always in the poorest parts of the communities. That was because immigrants had trouble getting good jobs due to their difficulty speaking proper English, their lack of education, and discrimination. As time went by, most immigrant groups were able to improve their social and economic conditions and move to better housing and improve their standing in their communities. However, one group was forced to keep living in the poor areas and as second-class citizens—African Americans. And in the 1960s, their anger over continuing racism that they believed was ruining their lives erupted into some of the worst rioting in U.S. history.

African American Riots

Between June 1963 and May 1968, at least 200,000 people participated in 239 urban riots across the nation that led to 8,000 injuries, 190 deaths, and hundreds of millions of dollars in damage. More than half of the riots were sparked by the April 8, 1968, assassination of civil rights leader Martin Luther King Jr. in Memphis, Tennessee. Riots in 125 cities in 28 states by blacks angry over his death claimed the lives of 46 people.

The riots all took place in ghettos, the run-down parts of cities in which most blacks lived. University of Oklahoma history professor Paul A. Gilje says blacks initiated the ghetto violence out of anger over the way blacks were treated in a society dominated by whites. He writes, "Blacks would vent pent up rage at an unresponsible justice and social system as well as economic exploitation in [waves of] looting, arson, and some assaults."[87] The anger was over discrimination against blacks in hiring, which kept them from getting better jobs, and in housing, which denied them the opportunity to buy or rent places to live in better neighborhoods.

Blacks also were angry over the racist way police treated blacks. Many riots began with a confrontation between black citizens and police that soon escalated into major violence because of mutual misunderstanding and long-standing hatred between the two sides. Blacks would unleash their pent-up anger over poverty and decades of police abuse by attacking police, damaging local businesses, and stealing items they could not afford to buy. Riots in the Watts section of Los Angeles from August 11 to August 16, 1965; in Newark from July 12 to July 17, 1967; and in Detroit from July 23 to July 30, 1967, all followed that pattern.

The six-day Watts riot, in which 34 people died; 1,032 were injured; and 3,952 were arrested, began on August 11, 1965, when white California Highway Patrol officer Lee Minikus arrested

Marquette Frye, an African American, for alleged drunk driving. A state report on the riot released December 2, 1965, claims the violence was caused by the long-standing black resentment toward police and their belief that racism was continuing to deny them the same opportunities whites had to obtain a decent life. The report states, "In examining the sickness in the center of our city, what has depressed and stunned us most is the dull, devastating spiral of failure [many blacks endure]. Equality of opportunity, a privilege [blacks] sought and expected, proved more of an illusion than a fact."[88]

Even blacks who had achieved some success participated in the riot. A college student told the commission investigating the Watts riot that his own anger about such past abuses made him feel ambivalent about what he had done. He said, "Well, you can say regret and then you say there are some who are glad it happened. Now, me personally, I feel that I regret it, yes. But, deep down inside I know I was feeling some joy while it was going on, simply because I am a Negro."[89]

Riots have struck many inner-city ghettos since then. One of the worst was the 1992 Los Angeles riot, which was sparked by the brutal beating Rodney King received from police on March 3, 1991, when he was arrested for a traffic violation. On April 29, 1992, four police officers were found innocent of charges connected with beating King. The verdict ignited several days of rioting in which fifty-three people died,

two thousand people were injured, and eleven hundred buildings were destroyed in a violent rampage of looting and destruction. The rioters were angry about more than King. One member of a youth gang explains, "[My] homies be beat like dogs by the police every day. This riot is about all the homeboys murdered by the police, about twenty-seven years of oppression. Rodney King just the trigger."[90]

The riots, however, did some good. Historians David Boesel and Peter H. Rossi claim that studies on why the 1960s riots happened showed "that far out of proportion to their numbers, blacks were at the bottom of the American class system."[91] As a result, government agencies began new educational and social welfare programs that helped blacks have better lives. And the 1992 riots forced Los Angeles to make changes in how its officers treated blacks.

Unlike riots sparked by real grievances, many episodes of urban violence simply seem to explode out of an excess of emotion over a trivial incident. Many of them involve young people.

Sports and Youth Riots

When the Los Angeles Lakers beat the Orlando Magic 99–86 in Los Angeles on June 14, 2009, to win their fifteenth NBA championship, twenty-one-year-old Ben Weiser put on his Lakers jersey and headed to the downtown area to celebrate with other fans. "I watched the last game at home but tonight I wanted to be where the action is,"[92] Weiser admitted. He joined thousands of other Lakers fans

"We Had a Revolt in Our Community"

Tommy Jacquette was twenty-one when he participated in the Watts riot in Los Angeles, California, in August 1965. Four decades later, Jacquette has no regrets about what he did. He explains:

> It's safe to say that I was throwing as many bricks, bottles and rocks as anybody. My focus was not on burning buildings and looting. My focus was on [one] of the most racist and most brutal [police] departments. People keep calling it a riot, but we call it a revolt because it had a legitimate purpose. It was a response to police brutality and social exploitation of a community and of a people, and we would no more call this a riot than Jewish people would call the extermination of the Jewish people "relocation." A riot is a drunken brawl at USC [University of Southern California] because they lost a football game. People said that we burned down our community. No, we didn't. We had a revolt in our community against those people who were in here trying to exploit and oppress us. We did not own this community. We did not own the businesses in this community. We did not own the majority of the housing in this community. Some people want to know if I think it was really worth it. I think any time people stand up for their rights, it's worth it.

Quoted in Valerie Reitman and Mitchell Landsberg, "Watts Riots, 40 Years Later," *Los Angeles Times*, August 11, 2005, www.latimes.com/news/printedition/la-me-watts11aug11,0,2014736.

who wanted to celebrate the victory. But as sometimes happens, the festivities got out of hand. Fueled by alcohol and high spirits, Lakers fans threw rocks and bottles at police trying to disperse them. They overturned police cars, started bonfires in the streets around the Staples Center where the Lakers played, and looted a gas station and stores. A similar riot occurred on June 20, 2000, when the Lakers won their last title.

A celebratory sports riot has become an ugly tradition in many professional and collegiate sports, like basketball, baseball, and hockey. On November 23, 2002, when Ohio State defeated archrival Michigan 14–9 in football, some five thousand revelers, many of them underage drinkers, partied on the Ohio State campus. In a drunken rage they flipped over twenty cars and started more than one hundred bonfires before police using tear gas broke up the rioting fans. Merrill J. Melnick, coauthor of *Sports Fans: The Psychology and Social Impact of Spectators*, believes alcohol is a major factor in celebrations gone wrong. He says:

> In sports psychology we call these things "celebratory riots." They are marked by a collective misbehavior when a large number of people are experiencing ecstasy and euphoria mixed in with large amounts of alcohol. These things tend to start off benign, with a lot of social milling. It doesn't take too much to get things going in a negative direction. It can start with a bonfire or a tipped-over car.[93]

High school– and college-age youths also have been involved in other riots involving seemingly senseless violence. On March 4, 2006, several hard-core punk bands, including G.B.H., the Addicts, Broken Bones, and Vice Squad, performed in

Several days of rioting occurred in Los Angeles, California, after four white police officers were found innocent of beating black motorist Rodney King in 1992. These riots resulted in the destruction of eleven hundred buildings, like this one.

Looting When the Lights Went Out

On July 13, 1977, a lightning strike caused most of New York City to lose power. During the blackout which lasted through the next day, many people took advantage of the darkness and looted more than sixteen hundred stores. People also set more than one thousand fires and committed other crimes. The following excerpt from an article in *Time* magazine describes the looting that occurred:

> Roving bands of determined men, women and even little children wrenched steel shutters and grilles from storefronts with crowbars, shattered plate-glass windows, scooped up everything they could carry, and destroyed what they could not. First they went for clothing, TV sets, jewelry, liquor; when that was cleaned out, they picked up food, furniture and drugs. [At] the Ace Pontiac showroom in The Bronx, looters smashed through a steel door and stole 50 new cars, valued at $250,000; they put the ignition wires together and drove off. Young men roamed East 14th Street in Manhattan, snatching women's purses. Adults toted shopping bags stuffed with steaks and roasts from a meat market on 125th Street in Harlem. "It's the night of the animals," said Police Sergeant Robert Murphy, who wore a Day-Glo blue riot helmet. "You grab four or five, and a hundred take their place. All we can do is chase people away from a store, and they just run to the next block, to the next store."

"The Blackout: Night of Terror," *Time*, July 25, 1977, www.time.com/time/magazine/article/0,9171,919089,00.html.

San Bernardino, California. Trouble began when fighting broke out after concertgoers began shouting racist slogans. The violence spilled out into the streets around the National Orange Show Events Center and about fifteen hundred of the four thousand concertgoers broke store windows and stole items, damaged cars, and set fires. After breaking windows at a Carl's Jr. restaurant, rioters entered and trashed the place. An employee at the restaurant, Socorro Garcia, said she and other workers, fearing for their lives, hid in the office. "Everything they could, they broke," Garcia said. "I was just hoping they wouldn't try to open [the office] door."[94] Rioters stole a cash register drawer and even a cardboard cutout of a cow. At the nearby Windjammer Gift Emporium, rioters took ten thousand dollars in merchandise after using a cement trash can to break security bars on the store's windows. Nearly two hundred police broke up the riot and arrested fifteen

The Woodstock Riot

Woodstock was the most famous concert in rock history. From August 15 to August 18, 1969, rock greats like Jimi Hendrix, Santana, the Grateful Dead, and the Who performed for an estimated half million people on a farm in Bethel, New York. There were no major problems with violence even though many in the huge crowd used marijuana and other drugs. But a thirtieth anniversary Woodstock concert held in Rome, New York, from July 23 to July 25, 1999, and attended by two hundred thousand people was not as peaceful. It is remembered for reports of rape, violence, and a premature ending thanks to riot conditions. Some historians believe the crowd was influenced by Limp Bizkit bandleader Fred Durst who had urged the audience to smash things. The following excerpt from an article in the *Philadelphia Inquirer* describes some of the violence that ended the concert:

> Hundreds of concertgoers fueled a dozen roaring fires with anything they could find: planks, frames, tables, tents. They toppled a lighting tower inside the former military base, and 20 of the most brazen scaled the twisted metal, singing "Give Peace a Chance." Flames engulfed 12 tractor-trailers after a propane explosion. Looters raided souvenir stands, turned over cars, and set one ablaze using "peace candles." "[It's] apocalypse now!" said Anthony Kiedis, lead singer of Red Hot Chili Peppers, before they closed their set with Jimi Hendrix's "Fire" [in a] prerecorded finale honoring Hendrix, the guitar hero who closed the first Woodstock.

Daniel Rubin, "On the Road to the Show," *Philadelphia Inquirer*, www.woodstock1999.com/news/story1012.html.

people on charges ranging from public drunkenness and burglary to assault with a deadly weapon.

Some college riots have started at on-campus social events. A riot erupted on April 25, 2009, at Kent State University in Akron, Ohio, during College Fest, an annual block party, when students began setting large fires in the street. Student Kristine Gill says, "The flames were filling the street, like 15 feet high, and kids were throwing furniture on it and hanging from trees and screaming 'KSU' [for Kent State University] over and over again."[95] Police in riot gear arrested about sixty people on various charges. University officials sent students an e-mail that said, "The university is disappointed in the events that have occurred and finds the behavior inexcusable."[96]

"Can We All Get Along?"

Kent State University's comment about student behavior could apply to all riots. So could a comment by Rodney King, who was the catalyst for the 1992 Los Angeles riot, which began because people were angry a jury had cleared four officers of beating him. On May 1, 1992, the third day of the intense rioting, King made a public appeal for an end to the violence. He said, "People, I just want to say, you know, can we all get along? Can we get along? Can we stop making it, making it horrible for the older people and the kids? It's just not right. It's not right."[97] King's words did little to stop the riot, but they summed up the cause of every riot in history—when people cannot solve their problems peacefully, they turn to violence.

Notes

Introduction: The Importance of Riots and Protests

1. Frederick Douglass, *Frederic Douglass: Selected Speeches and Writings*, Chicago, IL: Lawrence Hill, 1999, p. 367.
2. Ralph F. Young, *Dissent in America: The Voices That Shaped a Nation*, New York: Pearson Education, 2006, p. xxi.
3. Paul A. Gilje, *Rioting in America*, Bloomington: Indiana University Press, 1996, p. 1.
4. Quoted in Young, *Dissent in America*, p. xxi.

Chapter 1: Degrees of Dissent

5. Quoted in Michael Stone, "Death Threats Cancel Local Town Hall Health Care Meetings," *Portland (OR) Progressive Examiner*, August 9, 2009, www.examiner.com/x-4383-Portland-Progressive-Examiner~y2009m8d9-Death-threats-cancel-local-town-hall-health-care-meetings.
6. Quoted in Young, *Dissent in America*, p. xxii.
7. Henry David Thoreau, *The Variorum of Civil Disobedience*, New York: Twayne, 1996, p. 48.
8. Henry David Thoreau, "Resistance to Civil Government." Thoreau Reader. http://thoreau.eserver.org/civil.html.
9. Martin Luther King Jr., "I Have a Dream," speech, Washington Mall, Washington, DC, August 28, 1963. Transcript available at http://www.americanrhetoric.com/speeches/mlkihaveadream.html.
10. Quoted in Associated Press, "Santa Died for Your MasterCard," MSNBC, December 27, 2007, http://www.msnbc.msn.com/id/22373762/
11. Young, *Dissent in America*, p. xxii.
12. Richard C. Wade, *Urban Violence*, Chicago, IL: University of Chicago, 1969, p. 7.
13. Gilje, *Rioting in America*, p. 5.
14. Quoted in David D. Haddock and Daniel D. Polsby, "Understanding Riots," *Cato Journal* 14, no. 1 (Spring–Summer 1994), www.cato.org/pubs/journal/cj14n1-13.html.
15. Gilje, *Rioting in America*, pp. 7–8.
16. Quoted in David Boesel and Peter H. Rossi, *Cities Under Siege: An Anatomy of the Ghetto Riots, 1964–1968*, New York: Basic Books, 1971, p. 283.

Chapter 2: AntiGovernment Riots and Protests

17. Quoted in Richard Colton, "Shays Rebellion," National Park Service, www.nps.gov/spar/historyculture/shays-rebellion.htm.

18. Constitution of the United States, National Archives and Records Administration, www.archives.gov/exhibits/charters/constitution_transcript.html.

19. Bill of Rights, National Archives and Records Administration, www.archives.gov/exhibits/charters/bill_of_rights_transcript.html.

20. Quoted in John A. Garraty with Robert A. McCaughey, *The American Nation: A History of the United States to 1877*, vol. 1, 7th ed. New York: HarperCollins, 1991, p. 93.

21. Quoted in Howard Zinn and Anthony Arnove, *Voices of a People's History of the United States*, New York: Seven Stories, 2004, p. 81.

22. Page Smith. *A New Age Now Begins: A People's History of the American Revolution*, vol. 1, New York: McGraw-Hill, 1976, p. 251.

23. Douglas E. O'Neill, letter to the editor, *Argus Leader (Sioux Falls, SD)*, July 23, 2009, www.argus-leader.com/apps/pbcs.dll/article?AID=/200907230155/VOICES09/90723031.

24. Quoted in Gar Smith, "An Interview with Julia Butterfly Hill: Part 1," The-*Edge*, May 26, 2005, p. 1.

25. Quoted in "The Bonus Army," Eye-Witness to History.com, www.eyewitnesstohistory.com.

26. Quoted in Paul Dickson and Thomas B. Allen, "Marching on History," *Smithsonian*, February 2003, p. 84.

27. Quoted Sheryl Gay Stolberg, "Thousands Rally in Minnesota Behind Obama's Call for Health Care Overhaul," *New York Times*, September 13, 2009.

28. Quoted in *Milwaukee Journal Sentinel*, "Demonstrators Unite in Anger Toward President," September 13, 2009, p. A7.

29. Quoted in Thomas Bailey and David M. Kennedy, *The American Pageant: A History of the Republic*, vol. 8, 8th ed., Lexington, MA: D.C. Heath, 1987, p. 1,818.

Chapter 3: The Fight for Workers' Rights

30. Barack Obama, speech, AFL-CIO Labor Day picnic, Cincinnati, OH, September 7, 2009. Transcript available at www.huffingtonpost.com/2009/09/07/obama-labor-day-speech-at_n_278772.html.

31. Quoted in Howard Zinn, *A People's History of the United States*, New York: Harper and Row, 1980, p. 223.

32. "The Great Strike," *Harper's Weekly*, August 11, 1877. Also available at www.catskillarchive.com/rrextra/sk7711.html.

33. Quoted in Priscilla Murolo and A.B. Chitty, *From the Folks Who Brought You the Weekend: A Short, Illustrated History of Labor in the United States*, New York: The New Press, 2001, p. 151.

34. Gilje, *Rioting in America*, p. 145.

35. Quoted in Francis X. Donnelly, "UAW's Battles Shape History," *Detroit News*, September 16, 2008, http://detnews.com/article/20080916/AUTO01/809160319/0/AUTO01/UAW-s-battles-shape-history.

36. Cesar Chavez, "Cesar Chavez: In His Own Words," PBS, www.pbs.org/itvs/fightfields/cesarchavez4.html.

37. Quoted in Ralph W. Conant, *The Prospects for Revolution: A Study of Riots, Civil Disobedience, and Insurrection in Contemporary America*, New York: Harper and Row, 1971, p. 7.

Chapter 4: The Fight for Racial Equality

38. Boesel and. Rossi, *Cities Under Siege*, p. 285.
39. Quoted in James Mooney, "The Ghost-Dance Religion and the Sioux Outbreak of 1890," in *Fourteenth Annual Report of the Bureau of American Ethnology to the Secretary of the Smithsonian Institution 1892–93, Part 2*, by J.W. Powell, Washington, DC: Government Printing Office, 1896. Also available at www.pbs.org/weta/thewest/resources/archives/eight/wklakota.html.
40. Quoted in "Wounded Knee," *American Experience: We Shall Remain*, DVD, directed by Stanley Nelson, PBS, 2009. Transcript available at www.pbs.org/wgbh/amex/weshallremain/files/transcripts/WeShallRemain_5_transcript.pdf.
41. Quoted in Zinn, *A People's History of the United States*, p. 516.
42. Quoted in Ben Winton, "Alcatraz, Indian Land," *Native Peoples*, Fall 1999, p. 2.
43. Quoted in The History of Jim Crow Web site, "Incident," The History of Jim Crow Web site, www.jimcrowhistory.org/scripts/jimcrow/map.cgi?city=memphis&state=tennessee.
44. Eric Foner, *Reconstruction: America's Unfinished Revolution, 1863–1877*, New York: Harper and Row, 1989, p. 537.
45. Chicago Commission on Race Relations, *The Negro in Chicago: A Study of Race Relations and a Race Riot*, Chicago, IL: University of Chicago Press, 1922, p. 598.
46. Rosa Parks and Gregory J. Reed, *Quiet Strength: The Faith, the Hope, and the Heart of a Woman Who Changed the Nation*, Grand Rapids, MI: Zondervan, 1994, p. 26.
47. James Meredith, *Three Years in Mississippi*, Bloomington: Indiana University Press, 1966, p. 273.
48. Quoted in Herbert Apthecker, ed., *A Documentary History of the Negro People in the United States 1960–1968: From the Alabama Protests to the Death of Martin Luther King, Jr*, vol. 7, New York: Carol, 1994, p. 196.
49. Quoted in Young, *Dissent in America*, p. 286.
50. Quoted in Nhien Nguyen, "Remembering Vincent Chin," *International Examiner*, June 19 to July 2, 2002.
51. Quoted in Anita Hamilton, "A Day Without Immigrants: Making a Statement," *Time*, May 1, 2006, www.time.com/time/nation/article/0,8599,1189899,00.html.
52. Quoted in Dan Glaister and Ewen MacAskill, "US Counts Cost of Day Without Immigrants," *Guardian (England)*, May 2, 2006, www.guardian.co.uk/world/2006/may/02/usa.topstories3.

Chapter 5: The Fight for Gender and Sexual Orientation Equality

53. Quoted in Zinn and Arnove, *Voices of a People's History of the United States*, p. 458.

54. Quoted in Vern L. Bullough, *Before Stonewall: Activists for Gay and Lesbian Rights in Historical Context*, New York: Harrington Park, 2002, p. 7.

55. Quoted in Miriam Gurko, *The Ladies of Seneca Falls: The Birth of the Woman's Rights Movement*, New York: MacMillan, 1974, p. 307.

56. Quoted in Gurko, *Ladies of Seneca Falls*, p. 1.

57. Quoted in William Lavender and Mary Lavender, "Suffragists' Storm over Washington," *American History*, October 2003, p. 30.

58. Quoted in Elizabeth Williamson, "Sen. Clinton Draws Cheers Before Rally; Antiabortion Protesters Line March Route," *Washington Post*, April 25, 2004.

59. LifeChain.Net, home page, www.lifechain.net.

60. Quoted in Mark Thompson, ed., *Long Road to Freedom: The Advocate History of the Gay and Lesbian Movement*, New York: St. Martin's, 1994, p. 1.

61. Quoted in Lou Chibbaro Jr., "Gay Movement Boosted by '79 March on Washington," *Washington Blade*, November 5, 2004, www.washblade.com/2004/11-5/news/national/movement.cfm.

62. Quoted in Military.com, "AF Boots Decorated Pilot for Being Gay," Military.com, May 20, 2009, www.military.com/news/article/af-boots-decorated-pilot-for-being-gay.html.

63. Quoted in Mark Thompson, "'Don't Ask, Don't Tell' Turns 15," *Time*, January 28, 2008, www.time.com/time/nation/article/0,8599,1707545,00.html.

64. Quoted in Jennifer Dobner, "Gay Marriage Fight, 'Kiss-In' Protests Smack Mormon Image," Huffington Post.Com, August 16, 2008, www.huffingtonpost.com/2009/08/16/gay-marriage-fight-kiss-i_n_260535.html.

65. Laurel Thatcher Ulrich, *Well-Behaved Women Seldom Make History*, New York: Knopf, 2007, p. xiii.

Chapter 6: Opposing War

66. Quoted in Ray Raphael, *A People's History of the American Revolution: How Common People Shaped the Fight for Independence*, New York: The New Press, 2001, p. 163.

67. Quoted in Civil War Society, "New York City Draft Riots," in *The Civil War Society's Encyclopedia of the Civil War*, New York: Wings, 1997. Also available at www.civilwarhome.com/draftriots.htm.

68. Howard Zinn, "Opposing the War Party," *Progressive*, May 2004, www.progressive.org/may04/zinn0504.html.

69. Iver Bernstein, "July 13–16, 1863: The New York City Draft Riots," *Civil War Times*, August 2003, p. 34.

70. Quoted in Zinn, *A People's History of the United States*, p. 361.

71. Quoted in Young, *Dissent in America*, p. 286.

72. Quoted in Zinn, *A People's History of the United States*, p. 477.

73. Quoted "The Greatest Is Gone," *Time*, February 27, 1978, www.time.com/time/magazine/article/0,9171,919377-1,00.html.

74. James Johnson, David Samas, and Dennis Mora, press conference,

New York, June 30, 1966. Text available at www3.niu.edu/~td0raf1/history468/feb2603.htm.

75. Quoted in Thomas Oliphant, "I Watched Kerry Throw His War Decorations," *Boston Globe*, April 27, 2004, www.boston.com/news/globe/editorial_opinion/oped/articles/2004/04/27/i_watched_kerry_throw_his_war_decorations.

76 Quoted in Jennifer Schwall, "Only Vivid Memories Mark Antiwar Protests Here," *Wisconsin State Journal*, April 30, 1995.

77. Quoted in Neal Conan, "The Kent State Shootings, 35 Years Later," *Talk of the Nation*, transcript, May 4, 2005, www.npr.org/templates/transcript/transcript.php?storyId=4630596.

78. Quoted in Young, *Dissent in America*, p. 775.

79. Quoted in Tod Ensign, "Camilo Mejia Is Free: Conviction to Be Appealed," Citizen Soldier, www.citizen-soldier.org/CS07-Camilo.html.

80. Quoted in Associated Press, "Thousands Protest 6th Anniv. of Iraq War," CBS News, March 21, 2009, www.cbsnews.com/stories/2009/03/21/national/main4881873.shtml.

81. Quoted in Michelle Boorstein, V. Dion Haynes, and Allison Klein, "Dueling Demonstrations," *Washington Post*, September 16, 2007, p. A1.

Chapter 7: Urban Unrest

82. Wade, *Urban Violence*, p. 10.

83. Quoted in Zinn and Arnove, *Voices of a People's History of the United States*, p. 69.

84. Quoted in Zinn and Arnove, *Voices of a People's History of the United States*, p. 208.

85. Quoted in William D. Griffin, *The Book of Irish Americans*, New York: Random House, 1990, p. 146.

86. Quoted in *New York Times*, "South Omaha Mob Wars on Greeks," *New York Times*, February 22, 1909, p. 1.

87. Gilje, *Rioting in America*, p. 180.

88. Governor's Commission on the Los Angeles Riots, *Violence in the City: An End or a Beginning*? Governor's Commission on the Los Angeles Riots, December 2, 1965. Also available at www.usc.edu/libraries/archives/cityinstress/mccone.

89. Quoted in Ralph W. Conant, *The Prospects for Revolution: A Study of Riots, Civil Disobedience, and Insurrection in Contemporary America*, New York: Harper and Row, 1971, p. 45.

90. Quoted in Zinn and Arnove, *Voices of a People's History of the United States*, p. 564.

91. Boesel and Rossi, *Cities Under Siege*, p. 3.

92. Quoted in Associated Press, "At Least 25 Lakers Fans Arrested After Riot," June 15, 2009, FoxNews.com, www.foxnews.com/story/0,2933,526304,00.html.

93. Quoted in Thomas O'Toole, "Police Seek Ways to Curb 'Celebratory Riots,'" *USA Today*, April 9, 2002. p C11.

94. Quoted in Jeff Horwitz, "SB Picking up the Pieces," *San Bernardino Sun*, March 6, 2006, www.sbsun.com/search/ci_3572979.

95. Quoted in Paula Schleis, "Kent's College Fest Turns Rowdy," *Akron*

Beacon Journal, April 25, 2009, www
.ohio.com/news/break_news/
43705047.html.

96. Quoted in Ben Wolford and Kristine
Gill, "College Fest Ends in Riot,
Fires," *Daily Kent Stater*, April 24,
2009, http://media.www.kent-
newsnet.com/media/storage/
paper867/news/2009/04/24/
News/College.Fest.Ends.In.Riot.
Fires-3726211.shtml.

97. Quoted in LAist, "Rodney King: 17
Years After the Riots," LAist, April
29, 2009, http://laist.com/
2009/04/29/meet_rodney_king
.php.

For More Information

Books

Berkeley Art Center Association, *The Whole World's Watching: Peace and Social Justice Movements of the 1960s & 1970s*. Berkeley, CA: Berkeley Art Center Association, 2001. This book offers essays and many photographs about many protest movements of the 1960s and 1970s, including antiwar, gay rights, women's rights, and African American rights.

Herb Boyd, ed., *Autobiography of a People: Three Centuries of African-American History Told by Those Who Lived It*. New York: Doubleday, 2000. This book includes firsthand accounts of what it was like for civil rights workers to battle racism.

Dee Brown, *Bury My Heart at Wounded Knee: An Indian History of the American West*. New York: Holt, 1970. This history of Native Americans in the West is one of the best books ever written on the subject.

Tina Kafka, *Hot Topics: Gay Rights*. Detroit, MI: Lucent, 2006. This book offers a brief history of homosexuality and an overview of the gay rights movement for middle and high school students.

Stuart Kallen, *Women in History: Women of the 1960s*. Detroit, MI: Lucent, 2003. The book describes the sweeping changes that women experienced in the United States during the 1960s.

Clay Risen, *A Nation on Fire: America in the Wake of the King Assassination*. Hoboken, NJ: Wiley, 2009. A concise look at the violence that erupted in the wake of King's slaying.

Michael V. Uschan, *The 1960s Life on the Front Lines: The Fight for Civil Rights*. Detroit, MI: Lucent, 2004. This book details the various aspects of the Civil Rights fight in the tumultuous decade of the Sixties.

James Wilson, *The Earth Shall Weep: A History of Native America*. New York: Atlantic Monthly, 1998. This informative book covers the relationship between Native Americans and whites from the time the first colonists arrived.

Web Sites

American Memory (http://memory.loc.gov/ammem). A Web site of the Library of Congress, American Memory offers information about America, including articles, images, maps, sheet music, and sound recordings. One of its many collections is African American History.

Asian–Nation (www.asian-nation.org). This Web site offers information and photographs about all types of Asian Americans and links to other sites.

CenterLink (www.lgbtcenters.org). This Web site has links and information about lesbian, gay, bisexual, and transgender issues

Civil Rights Movement Veterans (www
.crmvet.org). This is a Web site about
people who fought for civil rights in
the 1950s and 1960s. It includes personal accounts, photographs, and
documents about that struggle.

National Organization for Women
(www.now.org). The National Organization for Women fights for women's
rights, and its Web site offers a history
of the organization and information
on issues concerning women.

Native American Sites (www.nativecul
turelinks.com/indians.html). This
Web site has many categories of information about individual Indian
tribes, languages, activities, and issues concerning Native Americans. It
also has links to other Native American sites.

Index

Vietnam Veterans Against the War
(VVAW), 80
Vietnam War protests, *11*
background, 76
bombings, 80
college campuses, 80, 81, *81*
Democratic National Convention, 22,
79, *79*
draft card burnings, *11*, 12
individuals setting selves on fire, 80
Moratorium to End the War,
74–75, 80
property destruction, 24
by soldiers, 78, 80
Violence
against African Americans, 13, 53,
75–76
against Bonus Army, 34–36, *35*
against Chinese Americans, 58–59
decrease in, 46
against homosexuals, 69
labor disputes, 43, *44*, 44–45
positive results from, 48
threats of, 15
against Vietnam war protesters, 22,
79, *79*, 80, 81, *81*
by Vietnam War protesters, 78, 80
against women's suffrage, 65–66
See also Riots
Voting rights
African Americans and, 53, 54
of German immigrants, 88
for Native Americans, 51
for women, *17*, 17–18, 64–66, *65*

W
Wade, Richard C., 22, 86
Walker report, 79
War, protests against
Iraq War, 20, 21, 32, 82, *83*, 83–85
Quakers, 74

U.S.-Mexican War, 18–19
See also Vietnam War protests
Washington Times (newspaper), 74
Waters, Walter W., 34
Watts riot, 90–91, 92
Weiser, Ben, 91–92
Wessel, Elaine, 66
Williams, Eugene, 53
Wilson, Woodrow, 45, 64, 65, 66
Wisconsin, University of, 80
Women
civil rights workers, 47, *47*, 55
position of, 63
textile workers, 41–42, *43*
Women's rights, fight for. *See* Gender
equality, fight for
Woodstock riot (1999), 95
Workers' rights, fight for
Ludlow Massacre, *44*, 44–45
property destruction, 24
protection for children workers, 40
tactics, 19, 45–46
by women, 41–42
women's equality, 67
See also Labor unions
World Trade Center, 82–83
World War I, 76
World War II, 76
Wounded Knee Massacre and
Occupation, 49–51, *51*
Wrentmore, Douglas, 81
Wyoming, 65

Y
Yasui, Minori, 57–58
Young, Ralph F., 12, 22
Youth riots, 24, 86, 91–95

Z
Zinn, Howard, 74
Zoot suit riots (1943), 60

Picture Credits

About the Author

Michael V. Uschan has written over seventy books, including *Life of an American Soldier in Iraq*, for which he won the 2005 Council for Wisconsin Writers Juvenile Nonfiction Award. Uschan began his career as a writer and editor with United Press International, a wire service that provided stories to newspapers, radio, and television. Uschan considers writing history books a natural extension of the skills he developed in his many years as a journalist. He and his wife, Barbara, reside in the Milwaukee suburb of Franklin, Wisconsin.

TOOLS FOR CAREGIVERS

- **F&P LEVEL:** B
- **WORD COUNT:** 31
- **CURRICULUM CONNECTIONS:** patterns, nature

Skills to Teach

- **HIGH-FREQUENCY WORDS:** a, has, have, many, one
- **CONTENT WORDS:** bee, beehive, butterfly, gardens, ladybug, patterns, spiderweb, sunflower
- **PUNCTUATION:** periods
- **WORD STUDY:** compound words (*beehive, butterfly, ladybug, spiderweb, sunflower*); long /e/, spelled ee (*bee, beehive*); long /e/, spelled y (*ladybug*); long /i/, spelled y (*butterfly*)
- **TEXT TYPE:** factual description

Before Reading Activities

- Read the title and give a simple statement of the main idea.
- Have students "walk" through the book and talk about what they see in the pictures.
- Introduce new vocabulary by having students predict the first letter and locate the word in the text.
- Discuss any unfamiliar concepts that are in the text.

After Reading Activities

Explain to readers that a compound word is two or more words joined together to create a new word. Have readers go back through the text. Ask them to point out the compound words they see. Then write each compound word on the board. Highlight the two words that make up each. Can readers name any other compound words?

Tadpole Books are published by Jump!, 5357 Penn Avenue South, Minneapolis, MN 55419, www.jumplibrary.com

Copyright ©2021 Jump!. International copyright reserved in all countries. No part of this book may be reproduced in any form without written permission from the publisher.

Editor: Jenna Gleisner   **Designer:** Michelle Sonnek

Photo Credits: Ian J Taylor/Shutterstock, cover; Marek Mierzejewski/Shutterstock, 1; JaySi/Shutterstock, 3; Hennadii_Havrylko/Shutterstock, 2bl, 4–5; Daniel Prudek/Shutterstock, 2tl, 6–7; Jag_cz/Shutterstock, 2tr, 8–9; Nor Gal/Shutterstock, 2br, 10–11; irin-k/Shutterstock, 2mr, 12–13; Parry Photography/Shutterstock, 2ml, 14–15; B.Forenius/Shutterstock, 16.

Library of Congress Cataloging-in-Publication Data
Names: Nilsen, Genevieve, author.
Title: Patterns in the garden / by Genevieve Nilsen.
Description: Minneapolis: Jump!, Inc., 2021. |
Series: Patterns in nature | Includes index. | Audience: Ages 3–6
Identifiers: LCCN 2020023438 (print) | LCCN 2020023439 (ebook) | ISBN 9781645277620 (hardcover)
ISBN 9781645277637 (paperback) | ISBN 9781645277644 (ebook)
Subjects: LCSH: Garden ecology—Juvenile literature. | Pattern Perception—Juvenile literature.
Pattern formation (Biology)—Juvenile literature.
Classification: LCC QH541.5.G37 N55 2021 (print) | LCC QH541.5.G37 (ebook) | DDC 577.5/54—dc23
LC record available at https://lccn.loc.gov/2020023438
LC ebook record available at https://lccn.loc.gov/2020023439

PATTERNS IN THE GARDEN

by Genevieve Nilsen

TABLE OF CONTENTS

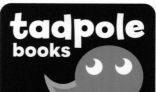

tadpole books

WORDS TO KNOW

bee

beehive

butterfly

ladybug

spiderweb

sunflower

IN THE GARDEN

Gardens have many patterns.

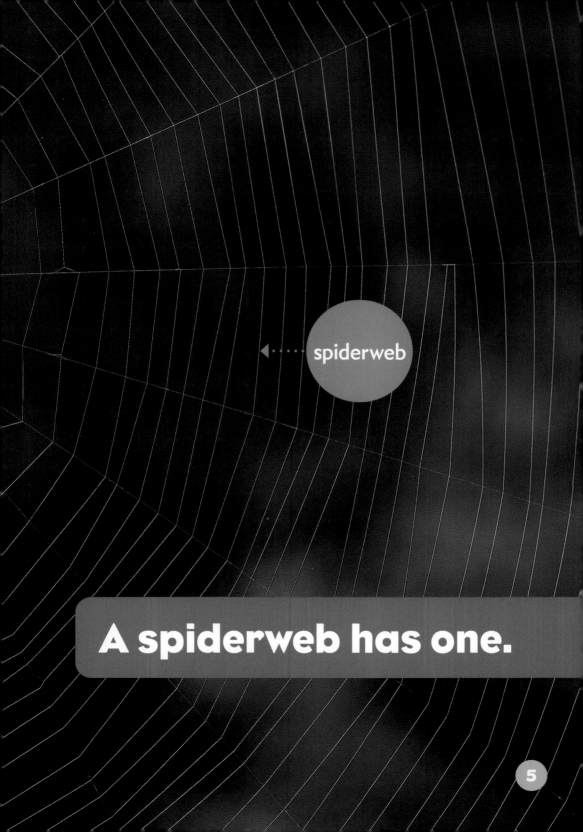

spiderweb

A spiderweb has one.

stripe

A bee has one.

honeycomb

A beehive has one.

seed

A sunflower has one.

spot

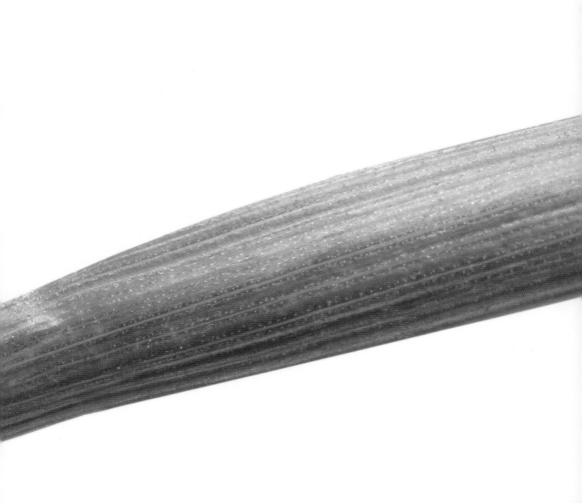

A ladybug has one.

A butterfly has one.

LET'S REVIEW!

A pattern is a design that repeats. What pattern do you see here?

INDEX

16